Thumbprint Mysteries

A CORPSE IN THE BASEMENT

BY

KATHLEEN ANNE BARRETT

CB

CONTEMPORARY BOOKS

a division of NTC/CONTEMPORARY PUBLISHING GROUP
Lincolnwood, Illinois USA

MORE THUMBPRINT MYSTERIES

by Kathleen Anne Barrett:

Measure Once, Kill Twice
Lethal Delivery, Postage Prepaid

Cover Design: Ellen Pettengell

ISBN: 0-8092-0643-9

Published by Contemporary Books,
a division of NTC/Contemporary Publishing Group, Inc.,
4255 West Touhy Avenue,
Lincolnwood (Chicago), Illinois 60646-1975 U.S.A.

890 QB 0987654321

CHAPTER 1

"I told you, I don't know where the body came from. Someone must have put it there when I wasn't home," I said.

Dave gave me an annoyed look and ran his hand through his hair. "Annie, why in the world would somebody put a dead body in your basement?" he asked.

"How should I know?" I said. "Are you telling me you don't believe me?" I was so surprised and hurt that I felt a lump form in my throat.

Dave rolled his eyes and let out a big sigh. "Of course *I* believe you. It's the police that I'm worried about. What are you going to tell them? How could you not have known he was there? Don't you ever go down there?"

"Of course I go down there," I said. "But I don't do it every day. I just didn't *see* it."

"But you must have smelled it," Dave said. "The

1

stench is really disgusting."

I was trying as hard as I could to keep my temper under control. True, it may have looked suspicious. But Dave was my best friend. I would've thought he'd trust me without question.

"I didn't notice the smell until last night," I said as I tightened my jaw. "And I just assumed it was a dead animal, like a rat. I didn't get up the courage to go downstairs and check on it until this morning. What's so hard to believe about that?"

"I don't know," Dave said. "I'm just wondering how it'll sound to the cops."

I gave Dave an angry glare as I snatched up my phone. I dialed 911 and stammered my way through an explanation. The police and the coroner showed up about twenty minutes later. They went straight to the basement without saying a word. On their way back up the stairs I heard the coroner say, "I'd guess he's been dead somewhere between thirty-six and forty-eight hours. That fruit cellar is pretty darned cold and that affects the state of the body some."

"Did you hear that?" Dave said to me in a loud whisper. "He could have been here for two days. How are you going to talk your way out of this one?"

I poked him in the ribs with my elbow. "Shh!" I said. "They'll hear you."

The detective was at the top of the stairs by that time. He walked into my kitchen and treated me to a cold, hard stare. Then he said, "Things don't look so good for you. A corpse doesn't just show up in a basement for no reason. Don't leave town. We'll find out who this is and be back to see you."

Believe me, that was a real treat.

*   *   *

My name is Annie Johnson, by the way. I live in Camden, New Jersey, and I've been here the entire thirty-four years of my life. So has Dave Barrio. We went to high school together. The first two years, we skipped out at least two days a week. When we turned sixteen, we dropped out altogether.

My mother certainly didn't care and neither did my teachers. It was pretty much the same for Dave, so we just hung out together and had a really good time for about a year. But then Dave's father died and he had to help support his mom and his little sister.

Nobody would hire him, of course, so he just did odd jobs for people. He'd do anything he could think of. He'd mow lawns, do landscaping, paint houses, repair things, and build stuff. If he didn't know how to do something, he'd keep trying until he figured it out. Today he has his own carpentry business. That's pretty darned impressive, if you ask me.

I never met my dad. My aunt Barb (my mom's sister) says he was such a deadbeat that we were better off without him. I'm not so sure, though. I always thought that it was my dad who started my mother drinking.

Mom had no money, no job, no education, and she was stuck with me. My aunt says my mom never felt that way. I know for a fact that she did, though. She told me over and over again that she never wanted me. She said I was the one who ruined her life, as if I had *asked* to be born or something. I really hated her for that. I hated her the most because, no matter how hard I tried, I couldn't make her love me. The last time I talked to her was over fifteen years ago.

When I was ten and the State sent me to live with my aunt, I swore I'd never grow up to be like my mother. I'd never drink, I'd never quit school, and I'd never go out with jerks like my father.

To this day, I still don't understand why I did all of that anyway. I drank more than she ever did. I quit school even younger than she did. And I went out with a string of guys who were so awful to me they'd probably make my dad look like an angel from heaven.

By the time I turned twenty, I was an alcoholic. I was still living with my aunt, but half the time I wouldn't even come home at night. One night, when I felt like I was really losing it, I went to see Dave. The next day, he took me to AA. He dragged me there, day after day, until I was finally willing to go by myself.

It took me over a year to stop wanting a drink. It took another five or six before I stopped being afraid I'd start again. Even now, almost ten years later, a trace of the fear is still there. Dave says it's a good fear, though. It's a fear that keeps me sober.

Two years and seven months after my first AA meeting, I got my GED. Then I started making crafts. They were just little things made out of wood with something painted on them. Dave taught me how to work with wood and how to use different saws. I don't have any real talent for drawing or painting, so I used stencils.

At first I sold things at flea markets. Today I sell at flea markets and craft fairs all over New Jersey and Pennsylvania. I also make things to order for three different stores in the area. I make a decent living and I'm taking care of myself. That's a lot more than I could ever say for my mom. Just a few months ago, I moved into the first house that I've ever owned. It's in pretty good shape and it's in a nice section of Camden.

*   *   *

Several days after the body was discovered, Dave

stopped by for breakfast. He does that every Sunday whether he's invited or not. After we'd finished eating, I took my phone book from the top of my refrigerator.

"What are you looking for?" Dave asked with a frown.

"A lawyer," I said. "I'm sure they're going to charge me with murder and I'm not going to just sit around and let them crucify me."

Dave closed the book on my fingers. "Forget the lawyers," he said. "They couldn't care less about you. All they want is your money. What you need to do is prove that you didn't do it."

I rolled my eyes. "And how in the world am I supposed to do that?" I said.

"You have to find out who the real killer is," he said.

I grabbed the book away from him. "So I'll hire a private detective."

He stopped me again and I glared at him. "Let me ask you something," he said. "Who usually handles all of your problems? Who do you rely on to take care of just about everything?"

I took a deep breath and slowly let it out. I felt like I was being given a test, and I wasn't enjoying it one single bit. "You?" I said, hoping I'd given the right answer.

Dave sighed and shook his head. "No, ding-dong. Not me, *you*. You are a very independent person, and no one deserves the credit for that but you."

I smiled at him. "You were an awful lot of help, you know. I hope you realize that."

Dave gave me a grateful look. I could see that he didn't completely accept what I was saying, though. "I may have given you a little guidance," he said, "but you did all the real work. You had to. That sort of thing can't be done for you. You have to do it yourself. No one but you can keep you from going for that bottle, am I right?"

I shrugged. "Yeah, you're right," I said. I was feeling a little self-conscious, so I asked, "Is there a point to all this? I thought we were trying to keep me out of prison. I doubt if they'll let me go because of my wonderful personality."

Dave smiled. "The point," he said, "is that we solve this murder ourselves. Forget the lawyers. Forget the detectives. It's just you and me."

I laughed out loud. "That's crazy," I said. "We don't know the first thing about solving murders. We don't know anything about that kind of stuff."

"We didn't know anything about carpentry or craft-making before we started those things either, did we?" he said with his eyebrows raised.

I thought about what he'd said for a few moments. Then I gave him a big smile. "Okay," I said. "You have yourself a partner. Where do we begin?"

Dave took a deep breath and pulled something from his pocket. "With this," he said in a voice clearly meant to warn me. I frowned at him and took hold of the letter he held in his hand. When I saw what it was, I just couldn't believe it. I didn't want to believe it. "Where did you get this?" I said in a shaky voice.

"I took it from his back pocket before the police came."

I dropped it on the table and put my face in my hands. "Oh, my God," I said. "How could I not have recognized him? How could I not have known it was him?"

"You didn't turn him over, remember? And you were too scared to take a close enough look."

I groaned and started shaking my head, my hands still covering my face.

"That's not all," Dave said. "Take a look at the obituary."

I looked at him with a sick expression as he handed me the newspaper. "Oh, my gosh," I said when I'd finished reading it. "Now what am I going to do? They're never going to believe I didn't do it."

CHAPTER 2

"Did you have any idea that he was married when you were going out with him?" Dave asked me.

"I had no idea at all," I said. Then I thought for a moment. "Of course, I guess I should have. He never took me to his place. We were always over here or out somewhere."

I put my head in my hands again. "God, I can't believe what a mess this is. I can just see the police report. First I was dating the dead guy they found in my basement. Then it turns out he was married the whole time I was seeing him. And, best of all, *he* broke up with *me* only a month before he was killed."

The dead guy's name was Hank Samuels. I had gone out with him for almost eight months. As far as I knew, there was no one else but me. Every time I thought there was, he told me I was imagining things. I've heard *that* story a few times before.

Dave sat down next to me and put his arm around my shoulder. "I know it looks bad," he said. "But don't worry, we'll figure it out. It has to be someone who knows both you and Hank."

I frowned. "Why do you say that?" I asked.

"Because they put him in your basement. Think about it. They had to know that you knew each other. It would be too much of a coincidence if they didn't."

"Good point," I said. "Now all I have to do is come up with a list of a hundred people who knew we were seeing each other."

Dave gave me a crooked smile. "It can't be that bad," he said. "Get some paper. We'll make a list."

I looked at him for a moment. Then I got up and found a pad of paper and a pen in my desk. When I sat down again, Dave leaned back in his chair. "Okay, who can you think of who knew about the two of you?"

"My aunt," I said.

Dave laughed. "Was she that picky about the guys you dated?" he asked.

"Not quite," I said with a smile. "I think we can rule her out."

"Okay, who else?" Dave said.

I took a deep breath and let it out. "Well, there was Paul Bolton. He worked with Hank, and he came with us to play pool a lot."

Dave wrote down his name. "Did they get along?" he asked.

"Sure, I guess. I never heard them argue about anything. Hank always wanted to invite him along. It was actually starting to get on my nerves. I felt like he wasn't satisfied just being with me."

Dave raised an eyebrow but didn't comment. "Where did you go to play pool?" he said.

"It was either BJ's Tap or Barb and Artie's. He liked to switch off. It was easier to hustle people that way. By the time we went back to the first place, they would have cooled down a bit. And there was always someone new to take in."

Dave sighed. "Every one of those people is a good possibility," he said. "Every guy he hustled and won money from could have had it in for him."

I nodded. "Yeah, they really did," I said. "BJ and Artie weren't too fond of him either. He was always upsetting their customers. They kept telling him he was hurting their business."

Dave just wrote down "pool players and bar owners" and left it at that. "We're going to have to go in and find as many of those people as we can," he said. "Okay, who else?"

I thought for a while. "Well, his boss, obviously."

Dave wrinkled his forehead. "How would he know about you?" he asked.

"Hank told him. And Hank had me invite him over for dinner. It was right after I bought the house."

"So they got along pretty well?"

"Yeah, it sure seemed that way," I said. "He was always giving Hank raises. He really liked his work."

"What was he working on? Who is this guy?"

"His name is Jeff Rogers," I said. "He's running the construction of that huge building downtown. Hank was already working that job when I met him. And it's not even close to being finished."

Dave nodded and scratched his head. "Do you think his wife knew about you?" he asked.

"How should I know?" I said. "I didn't even know about her until you showed me the obituary. I didn't know about his son or his sister either."

"How about his mom? Did you ever meet her?"

"Nope," I said. "I doubt that he was in a big hurry to introduce us. What was he supposed to say? 'This is Annie, my girlfriend'?"

Dave laughed. "Good point," he said. Then he frowned. "Didn't he have any friends besides Paul?"

I thought for a moment. "Yeah, I think he did. He mentioned some guy named Joe a couple of times. I don't know his last name, though."

"Well, maybe he'll be at the viewing. Or maybe his wife will know who he is."

I smirked at him. "Oh, right. Like we're going to just walk up and introduce ourselves. 'Hi, I'm your dead husband's old girlfriend. Do you mind if I ask you some questions?' I don't think that will go over too well, do you?"

Dave shook his head. "I was planning to be a little more subtle," he said. "We don't need to tell them who you are. Or at least we don't need to tell them about you and Hank. Maybe we can just say that I was a good friend of his. We could even pretend that you're going out with me."

I laughed so loudly that I think it hurt Dave's feelings. I could see it in his face.

"I didn't mean that the way it sounded," I said. "I just think the whole idea of playing detective is kind of funny, don't you?"

"It's going to be interesting, I'll tell you that. We're going to have our work cut out for us. There's no reason why any of these people will want to talk to us. They may just tell us to get lost."

I smiled. "Don't worry about that," I said. "I can get just about anyone to tell me anything."

Now Dave burst out laughing.

"I'm serious," I said. "I always could. My aunt used to say I had the magic touch. People just feel right at home with me. I make them feel comfortable. Once they start talking to me, they tell me all kinds of things. Really personal stuff too. Sometimes it can get kind of weird."

Dave laughed again. "This I've got to see," he said. Then he frowned. "I wonder if he had any other girlfriends."

I glared at him.

"Sorry," he said. "We do have to consider that, you know. I hate to ask you this, but why did he say he was breaking up with you?"

I picked up the pen Dave had put on the table. Then I started to doodle on the pad.

"Annie," Dave said in a kind voice. "What did he tell you?"

I sighed. "He said he wanted us both to see other people. He said I was crowding him. He felt trapped. He needed some space. All the usual lines every woman I've ever known has heard a million times."

Dave winced.

"Well, it's true," I said. "Now be honest. Haven't you said the same sort of thing to at least a dozen women at some time or another?"

Dave's face actually got a little pink. I took that as a yes, even though he quickly said, "I have one more thing to tell you."

I frowned and waited for him to continue.

"Hank came to see me right after he broke up with you."

"What?" I said in a loud and angry voice. "Why didn't you tell me that? What did he say?"

The answer Dave gave me just made the whole thing about ten times more confusing. It also gave me even more to worry about.

CHAPTER 3

The viewing was held the next night and Dave and I went together. I have to tell you, I was really nervous. Some of the people there would know me and that could cause a problem. Hank's wife would almost surely see me talking to Paul and Jeff Rogers. She was going to be very curious about who I was.

When we walked in, I was surprised to see how many people were there. I actually recognized quite a few of them. I saw Paul right away. He walked over to me and I introduced him to Dave.

Paul shook his head. "I just can't believe this happened," he said. "Why would anyone want to kill Hank?"

I gave Paul a sad look. "I don't know," I said, "but Dave and I are planning to find out."

Paul wrinkled his brow. *"You're* going to find out?" he said. "Why don't you just let the police take care of it?"

"Because she's their prime suspect," Dave said. "We can't afford to rely on the police."

Paul gave me a strange look. "Yeah, I heard he was found in your basement," he said. Then he just stared at me and waited for me to answer.

I sighed. "Yes, Paul. He was. But I didn't kill him. I don't know how he got there."

"We figure it had to be someone who knew about Annie and Hank," Dave said. "Do you have any ideas?"

Paul looked at me and frowned. "Plenty of people knew," he said. "You came to the site almost every week. Anyone could have seen you."

I groaned. "You're right," I said. "I forgot about that." Then I thought for a moment. "Do you think Jeff Rogers would let us come and talk to the guys sometime?"

Paul let out a small laugh. "I really don't know. You'll have to ask him. But don't expect him to be all that helpful. He's not that kind of guy. He really doesn't like people hanging around the site. He's been cracking down more than ever lately."

I looked around the room. Then I spotted Jeff Rogers. I took hold of Dave's arm. "No time like the present," I said. "I'll talk to you later, Paul."

I pulled Dave along with me and caught Jeff before he had a chance to start talking to someone else. "Jeff," I said. He turned around, took a deep breath, and smiled.

"Annie," he said. "How are you?" He had that look about him that told me he thought I was guilty. I clenched my teeth.

"I'm fine," I managed to say. Then I introduced Dave. "I'm sure you know Hank's body was found in my basement," I said.

Jeff nodded and just kept staring at me. I was starting to feel very irritated as well as insulted.

"He was put there," I said in a voice that let him know how I felt. "And we think he was put there by someone who knew I was going out with him."

Jeff spread his hands and shrugged.

"We'd like to come and talk to you sometime," Dave said. "I know you're very busy but this is important. Don't you agree?"

Jeff sighed and then nodded. It was pretty hard to say no to that. "I'll talk to you now if you want," he said.

I opened my mouth to say something but Dave cut me off. "I'd rather make it another time," he said. "This really isn't the right place. I'd hate for his family or friends to hear us."

Jeff nodded. "You're right," he said. "Stop by on Wednesday if you like. But make it after five. I'll be pretty tied up until then."

"That would be fine," I said and Dave agreed. "We'll see you then. Thank you very much, Jeff."

Jeff gave me a friendly smile. "You're very welcome," he said.

When we turned around, I saw that Paul had been watching us. When he saw me looking at him, he turned away. I frowned. "Let's go talk to Paul again," I said. But Dave wasn't listening. He was watching a woman dressed all in black, clinging to a man's arm. The man looked to be in his mid- to late thirties. The woman was crying and he was stroking her hair.

"I wonder if that's his wife and son," Dave said.

I winced. I felt a mixture of pity and guilt as well as jealousy.

"Come on," Dave said. "Just follow my lead."

I started to pull back but he took my arm. "Don't worry," Dave said. "It'll be all right."

When we reached them, Dave gave her a kind look. The man tried to smile and the woman just stared. Dave held out his hand to the man. "I'm Dave Barrio," he said. "I was a good friend of Hank's. This is my wife, Annie." I almost choked but I managed to make it look like a cough.

"I'm Harry," the man said. "Hank was my dad. This is my mom."

I held out my hand to her and she took it. "I'm really sorry, Mrs. Samuels. I knew Hank and I thought he was very nice."

She smiled warmly. I felt like such a jerk. But what could I do? To tell her the truth would have been so cruel. I just couldn't do it.

Dave looked at Harry. "Could we talk to you for a few minutes?" he asked.

Harry looked a little unsure but then he said yes. He took Mrs. Samuels to a chair and came back over to us.

"I'm sorry about that," Dave said. "I really need to talk to you about something. But I was afraid it would upset your mother."

Harry nodded. "Thank you," he said. "She's upset enough as it is."

Dave swallowed hard. "We have a problem," he said. "Your father's body was found in Annie's basement."

Harry stepped back a bit and stared at Dave with his mouth open. Then he gave me the same sort of look. "So you're the one," he said.

I wasn't sure what he meant by that so I kept quiet.

"Your father and Annie were friends," Dave said. "We don't know why he was put in her basement. But we plan to find out because it makes her look guilty."

Harry's eyebrows went up and he gave me a funny look. I took a deep breath and sighed. "I didn't kill him," I said. "Really, I didn't. I liked him. He was a good friend."

Harry sucked in his cheeks and looked away. Then he moved his head in the direction of a group of people. "Do you see that woman over there?" he said. "The one in the blue dress?"

I nodded.

"She was *really good friends* with my dad too." He turned to look at me again. He knew about us. I could see it in his face. I sighed again.

"How long were you seeing him?" Harry asked me.

I blushed and looked at Dave. Dave shrugged and gave me a comforting smile.

"About eight months," I said. "But we broke up about a month before he died," I quickly added.

"Who ended it?" Harry said in a cold voice.

I opened my mouth but Dave broke in. "Your father ended it," Dave said. "but there were no hard feelings between them. And he did it for a reason I think you'll understand. He came to see me after they broke up and he told me why he ended it. Annie didn't know about your mother until after your father was killed. But your dad told me that he ended it because of your mother. He wanted to make his marriage work. At least he wanted to give it a shot. He knew he couldn't do that and see other women at the same time."

Harry looked at me and I looked down at the floor.

"I didn't tell Annie about what your dad told me

until last night. Your dad made me promise not to tell her. He felt like he needed to explain it to someone. But I think he was afraid that if he told Annie, he might change his mind."

Harry was staring across the room at his mother with a sad look on his face. I wanted to say something to make him feel better, but I didn't know what to say.

"Who is the other woman?" Dave asked him.

Harry turned and looked at us. "Her name is Melissa Jorgensen. My dad was fooling around with her for over five years. She didn't know about my mom either, until about a month ago. He broke up with her too."

I felt sick to my stomach. I just couldn't believe it. All those months I was seeing Hank, he was also seeing Melissa. And he broke up with both of us at about the same time.

"Does your mother know?" I asked in a weak voice.

Harry stared at me for a few moments. "What do you think?" he said. "My mom's no idiot. She never said a word to my dad, but I'm sure she knew what was going on. I could see it every time she looked at him. He gave her one stupid excuse after another, every night of the week. I don't know who he thought he was fooling."

Me, for one, I thought to myself. Then I looked across the room and saw someone watching me. It was one of the detectives who had been at my house. I gave him a weak smile but he didn't smile back. Then he came over and told me he needed to talk to me. He scared me half to death. It was one of those nights I'll never forget.

CHAPTER 4

After the detective was finished with me, Dave put his arm around my shoulders. "Detective Foster. What a tactful guy," Dave said in a sarcastic voice. "I can't believe he questioned you here at the viewing. The least he could have done was wait until after the funeral."

I rested my head on Dave's shoulder. "I still can't believe he's thinking about charging me with murder," I said. "What am I going to do?"

Dave gave me a hug. "First you have to calm down. You're not thinking straight because you're too scared. We'll figure this out, I promise you. We can do anything, remember?"

I smiled and even laughed a little. That was our favorite phrase, especially when we were in our twenties. *We can do anything.* When we were kids, we'd always thought we were such failures. But after we quit school, we had to take care of ourselves. And we proved, time after time, that we could. We could do just about anything we wanted if we tried hard enough.

"You're right," I said. "We need to talk to everyone we can find. We'll find out everything we can about Hank. He kept some pretty big secrets from me. I wouldn't be surprised if there's a lot more that I don't know about him."

"Now you're talking," Dave said. "Let's get out of here. The funeral is tomorrow morning at eight o'clock. I'd really like to get some sleep."

*   *   *

After Dave dropped me off, I sat up for hours, making notes on a pad of paper. I wrote down everything I could think of. People Hank and I had met. Conversations I could remember. Things he had said that didn't make sense. I didn't solve anything by doing it, but it got me thinking.

Hank spent an awful lot of time at bars playing pool. I used to get so annoyed because that was the only place he'd take me. I ate most of my meals at the bar while he hustled the other pool players. He was so good at it.

He'd drink ginger ale all night long, but he'd pretend it was whiskey. He'd act only a little drunk at first. Then he'd pretend to get more and more drunk as the night wore on.

He'd play pool the whole time. At first he'd shoot about average. But as he pretended to get more and more drunk, he'd play worse every game. He wouldn't even suggest a bet until he looked like he was really drunk. Almost anyone would fall for it. It even worked with a lot of the guys he'd played with before. His act was so good that most of them never figured out that he was sober.

He'd act like the bet sort of pumped him up. He tried to make it look like that was the reason he was able to win after playing so badly all night. But every once in a while, someone would figure it out. And sometimes it got a little scary.

There was one guy who dragged him out back by his shirt. When the guy came back in, Hank wasn't with him. I found him on the ground with a face full of blood. He wasn't hurt very badly but it scared me an awful lot.

That wasn't the only time something like that happened. At least once a month somebody would get really angry. There was almost always a fight. Sometimes it was right in the bar. Sometimes it was outside. I begged Hank to stop doing it. He wouldn't listen to me, though. He said it was part of the challenge. Sometimes you win. Sometimes you lose. He really seemed to enjoy it. It sure didn't look like much fun to me.

A lot of those guys were regulars at Barb and Artie's or BJ's Tap. I didn't know any of their names. But I might be able to find out from the bar owners. Barb and Artie's was Hank's favorite place. Barb died over fifteen years ago but Artie kept the place going. And he never changed the name. I liked that. I thought it was sweet.

Of course, Artie knew that Hank was faking the whole thing. Artie was the one who was giving him the ginger ale. The same was true for BJ. Neither one of them was pleased with Hank. They both threatened to kick him out for good. But neither of them ever did it. He caused an awful lot of trouble in their bars. But I think he may have been good for their business too. He kept people hanging around. And when they hung around, they bought more drinks.

*   *   *

The next morning, I was really tired. I had stayed up way too late. And I hadn't slept well, either. I couldn't get it off my mind. They were going to charge me with murder, and there was a ton of evidence against me.

I put on a dark gray dress and waited for Dave to pick me up for the funeral. When he saw my face, he gave me a warm smile. "Come on," he said. "Let's get this over with. You'll feel a lot better after we get back."

Dave helped me with my coat and we rode to the church in silence. I didn't feel like talking. There was nothing to say.

Everyone I had seen at the viewing was also at the funeral. Even the detective was there. Mrs. Samuels cried openly. She was sitting between Harry and a woman who I guessed was Hank's sister. Harry had a hard look to him. He showed no emotion at all. Melissa Jorgensen showed no emotion either. I found that very surprising.

After the service, I walked up to Melissa and introduced myself. I had decided the night before to tell her who I was. I figured that was the best way to get her to talk to me. She might feel we had something in common.

"So you're the little tramp," was the first thing she said. I wasn't ready for that. I really wanted her to talk to me so I had to think fast.

I gave her a kind smile. "I'm really sorry, Melissa. If I had known about you or about Mrs. Samuels, I never would have been with Hank."

That seemed to calm her down a little. She shrugged and looked away. "Yeah, I didn't know about his wife either," she said quietly.

"When did you find out?" I asked.

"Last month. He told me he was leaving me for her. It's almost funny when you think about it. How many men leave their girlfriends for their wives?"

I laughed. "Not too many, I'll bet. I guess we just got lucky. He left me for the same reason. But in my case, he didn't bother to tell me. He told my best friend instead. I didn't find out why he broke up with me until a couple of nights ago. And I didn't know about his wife until I read the obituary."

Melissa gave me a caring look. "That was an awful way to find out. I'm sorry you had to go through that."

"Thanks," I said with a smile. She didn't seem so bad after all.

"I don't know if you know this," I said. "But they're going to charge me with Hank's murder. It's because he was found in my basement. And because I was going out with him."

Melissa's eyes widened. "The body was in your basement?" she said. "That doesn't look good."

"Tell me about it," I said. "I have to find out who did it. It's the only way I'm going to get out of this. The police aren't interested in proving my innocence."

Melissa raised her eyebrows. "How do you plan to do that?" she said.

"Well, the first step is to talk to everyone I can find. I need to find out as much as I can about him."

Melissa frowned.

"I know that sounds funny," I said. "But he wasn't honest with either of us. There's no telling what other secrets he might have had."

Melissa nodded. "You're right," she said. "I hadn't thought of that. I'd like to help you if I can. But I don't know what I can do. As you said, he wasn't honest with either of us."

"Yes, but he may have told each of us different things.

And you knew him so much longer than I did. I was only with him for eight months."

Melissa sighed. "Okay, what would you like me to do?"

"Just get together with me sometime. I'd like to talk to you about him. I know it's a touchy subject. And I know it may be hard to talk to me about it. But I really need to know everything you can tell me about him. What was he like? What did you do together? What did he talk about? And I'd like to do it as soon as possible. I don't have a lot of time."

Melissa nodded. "How about tomorrow night?" she said. "I live at 1750 Mercer Lane, apartment 304. You could stop by around eight. Would that be all right?"

I gave her a grateful smile. "That would be wonderful," I said. "Thank you so much, Melissa."

"You're quite welcome," she said.

Dave motioned to me as I was walking away from Melissa. "Let's go home," he said when I reached him. "This is too depressing."

Dave handed me my coat and we walked toward the door. As we were leaving, I saw Melissa watching me. The look on her face surprised me a little. But it didn't surprise me nearly as much as our meeting the next night.

CHAPTER 5

The next day and night were busy. I had a craft fair that day and Dave was busy with his own work. We didn't get together until four-thirty. Then we left to see Jeff Rogers, Hank's old boss, at five.

A lot of the men were still on the job. The building looked finished from the outside. The parking lot and sidewalks were completed too. But the inside had a long way to go.

Paul was there and he waved when we came in. Dave and I walked over to meet him.

"If you're here to see Rogers, you may be better off coming back another time," he said. "This was one hell of a day."

I sighed. "So he's in a bad mood?"

"He's always in a bad mood," Paul said with a laugh. "But today he's worse than usual."

I knew Paul was just trying to be funny, but I was sorry we hadn't chosen another day. It's hard to get someone to talk when he's in a bad mood. Just as I was about to suggest to Dave that we come back some other time, Jeff walked over and held out his hand.

"Annie, Dave, glad to see you. Come on back to my office. It's pretty dirty but at least it's private."

Paul shrugged as I shook Jeff's hand. Dave and I followed Jeff to his office. It was covered with a gray powder and it made me cough.

"Sorry about the dust," Jeff said. "You get used to it after a few months."

I smiled and so did Dave. Dave took a seat on the edge of a box. Jeff offered me a chair after he cleaned it off. "So what can I do for you?" he asked us. "I knew Hank a long time. He's really missed around here. His work was first-rate."

I nodded. "He really appreciated all the raises you gave him," I said. Jeff stiffened a bit when I said that but then he relaxed.

"He deserved every one of them," Jeff said. "I believe in treating my boys right. When they work hard, they get paid for it."

"Did Hank have any trouble with anyone who worked here?" I asked.

Jeff frowned. "Trouble?" he said. "I'm not sure what you mean."

"Was there anyone that he didn't get along with? Did you ever hear him argue with anyone?"

Jeff thought for a while. "Now that you mention it, I did hear something. One night when a few of us were working late, Hank got into a fight with one of the men. The guy's name was Fred Matthews."

"Do you know what they were fighting about?" Dave asked.

Jeff shook his head. "I couldn't tell," he said. "I wasn't close enough to hear much of what they said. They were both pretty hot, though. At one point, I was afraid I'd have to break it up."

"Is Fred Matthews here right now?" I said.

Jeff paused just a moment before he answered. "No," he said. "Fred doesn't work here anymore. He called me the morning after he and Hank had the fight. He said he was quitting. I asked him to give me time to replace him, but he refused. These people don't realize how hard it is to run a project like this. They have no idea how much trouble something like that can cause."

Dave nodded. "I know what you mean," he said. "Can you tell us how to reach Fred Matthews?"

Jeff shook his head. "I'm sorry, I can't give out that kind of information. Company policy."

"Is there anyone here who might know how to reach him?" I said. "Was he friendly with anyone?"

Jeff let out a bitter laugh. "Yeah. He was friendly with Hank until that night. I don't know how well he knew anyone else."

"Would you mind if we came back during the day?" I asked. "I'd really like a chance to talk to some of the guys."

Jeff took a deep breath and slowly let it out. "I'm sorry," he said. "I can't do that. As you can see, I have a big job to get done. That sort of interruption could set me way back. You'll have to see the men on their own time."

I nodded. "I understand," I said. "Would it be all right if we came in just to make arrangements to see them?"

Jeff closed his eyes and sighed. "All right," he said. "But

come during the lunch hour. We break from twelve to one. Now if you'll excuse me, I really have to get back to work."

Jeff stood up, so Dave and I did too. We had taken a lot of his time and I knew he was busy. "I really appreciate your talking to us, Jeff," I said. "I hope we haven't caused you any trouble."

Jeff smiled broadly. "No trouble at all," he said. "I'm glad to help. Hank was more than an employee to me. He was a friend. You know that."

I nodded. "Yes, I do. Thanks, Jeff."

As we were walking out, Paul waved us over. "Did he talk to you?" he asked me.

"Yeah, he was pretty helpful," I said. "And he said we could stop by and talk to everyone during your lunch break some day."

Paul raised his eyebrows and shook his head. He still had a puzzled look on his face when we said goodbye.

"Next appointment: Melissa Jorgensen," Dave said when we reached his car. "Let's get something to eat before we go to see her."

I gave him an anxious look. "I was hoping you wouldn't mind if I saw Melissa by myself," I said. "I think I might be able to get her to talk more if I go alone."

Dave sighed. "You may be right," he said. Then he gave me a curious smile. "Do you think she could have done it?"

I laughed. "I suppose so," I said, "but I have no reason to believe that she did."

"She didn't shed a tear at the viewing or the funeral," Dave said.

I thought about that for a few moments. "I know," I said. "I noticed that. But she could be holding back. A lot of people do that. It's the only way they can handle something so painful."

"Maybe," Dave said. "But it does make you wonder."

We stopped at a McDonald's and ate inside. Dave ordered his usual large fries, double cheeseburger, large Coke, and two apple pies.

"What did you think of the Fred Matthews story?" Dave said after he'd finished his first pie. "Where do you think the guy is?"

I shrugged. "Well, I have two theories," I said. "One, he killed Hank and ran off to avoid getting caught. Two, he moved on to another part of the state or the country. And he's probably doing the same sort of work there that he was doing for Rogers. I'd love to know what they were arguing about, though. Jeff said there were some other guys around when it was happening. Maybe we should go back tomorrow and see if we can find them."

"I can't go tomorrow," Dave said. "I have to work. But I was thinking we might stop in and see Hank's son tomorrow night. We could pay him a surprise visit. You never know what we might catch him doing."

I laughed. "What do you think we're going to catch him doing? Burying the gun? What possible motive could Harry have for killing his own father?"

Dave shrugged. "Revenge for his mother. He knew all about Hank's affairs, you know. And he had known for a long time. He didn't seem to appreciate the effect it had on his mother."

I gave Dave a grim look. "That's true," I said.

*   *   *

Thirty minutes later, I pulled up in front of Melissa Jorgensen's apartment. I was almost an hour early but I was hoping she'd be home. I don't know what made me go before the agreed time. It was just a hunch, I guess. Dave's idea about catching someone off guard must have had an effect on me.

It was already dark outside and only a few lights were on in the building. There was no security lock so I walked right in. I climbed the two flights of stairs to the third floor and knocked on number 304. For several minutes, no one answered. I heard muffled voices soon after I knocked and a lot of movement inside. Then Melissa opened the door. She was wearing a satin robe tied at the waist. The colors were ugly—bright purple, green, orange, and red all mixed together. Her hair was a mess, and she had lipstick smeared on her face. I gave her a funny smile.

"I guess I'm a little early," I said. "I was already in the neighborhood so I thought I'd take a chance." A stupid excuse, but what else could I say?

"Can you come back at eight?" she said. Her voice was unfriendly and so was her expression.

"Oh, just let her in," a man said. The man's voice was familiar, but I couldn't quite place it. When Melissa shrugged and opened the door to let me in, I just stared in disbelief.

CHAPTER 6

"Harry?" I said with wide eyes. I looked from Harry to Melissa and back again. "What are you doing here?"

Melissa rolled her eyes, let out a little laugh, and leaned against her couch. Harry took a deep breath and coughed. Neither of them said a word.

I wasn't sure what to say, either. I decided to use the direct approach. "So how long has this been going on?" I asked. I didn't get an answer right away so I kept quiet and waited.

Finally Melissa sighed and looked at Harry. "Tell her, Harry," she said. "What's the use? She's going to find out anyway. Everyone's going to know sooner or later."

Harry pursed his lips. "It's none of your business," he said to me. "But Melissa's right. You'll find out one way or another so I may as well tell you. It's been going on for almost a year."

I raised my eyebrows. "Did your dad know?" I asked.

Harry laughed. "He'd have killed us both if he'd known," he said. "No, he never suspected a thing. Would you?"

I really didn't have an answer for that one so I ignored it. I turned to Melissa. "And this was happening while you were still going out with Hank?" I said.

She shrugged. "Hey, don't knock it. Hank was married and he was seeing you."

"Yeah, but you didn't know that," I said. When she didn't respond, I frowned. "Or did you?" I asked.

She sighed a heavy sigh. "I told you. I didn't know about his wife until last month. I didn't know about you until a few days before I met you."

There was something very wrong with this picture. I frowned at Melissa. "If you didn't know about Hank's wife, who did you think Harry was?"

They both burst out laughing at the same time. "She thought my dad was divorced," Harry said.

I couldn't believe what I was hearing. "So instead of telling her about your mom, you decided to have an affair with her too?" I said in a screechy voice.

Melissa turned down both corners of her mouth and glared at Harry. He gave her an impatient look. "What difference did it make?" he said to me. "She knew I wasn't married, and she was cheating on Dad. None of us was exactly innocent."

I laughed and shook my head. I'd heard enough about that for the time being. I sat in a chair across from the couch. They hadn't asked me to sit down but I didn't care. "Are you still willing to talk to me?" I said to Melissa.

"Sure. Why not?" she said.

"How about you?" I said to Harry.

He sighed. "Yeah, but let's make it another time. I think this is my cue to leave."

That was the response I was hoping for. I really didn't want to talk to them both at the same time. Melissa walked Harry to the door and stepped outside with him for a few moments. When she came back in, she was smiling.

She sat down on the couch, crossed one leg over the other, and watched me. I stared right back. "Tell me the truth, Melissa. What made you start up with Harry?"

She raised one eyebrow. "Money," she said. "And lots of it. Hank's darling son has a small fortune."

"From what?" I said.

"Cement," she said. "His grandfather left it to him. He passed Hank over because he didn't trust him. He thought Hank would run the company into the ground and blow all the money."

"How do you know this?" I asked.

"From Hank," she said. "It happened just last year. Hank's dad died of cancer. I knew about the cement business all along. Hank was sure he'd inherit it. He was just biding his time until the old man died."

I stared at the floor for a few moments. Hank had never said a word to me about any of that. But then we'd only been seeing each other for eight months. It must have happened before we met. "How did Hank feel when it happened?" I said. "Was he angry?"

"Angry?" Melissa said. "He was furious. And not just at his father. He was furious with Harry too. He felt like Harry had stolen it away from him. He really believed he had a right to that business. I kind of understood how he felt. He did get a raw deal when you think about it."

She was really something. She'd started cheating on Hank as soon as Harry got the cement business. But now she was telling me she felt sorry for Hank because he got a raw deal. She sure had gone out of her way to make him feel better, hadn't she?

"Does Harry know why you're interested in him?" I said. "It had to have been pretty obvious. He inherits a fortune and suddenly you're all over him."

Melissa sneered at me. "Let's not get nasty, dear. You would have done the same thing in my position."

I laughed. "I certainly would not," I said. "I never thought Hank had any money to begin with. And I never cared."

Melissa looked at me as if I were a childish idiot. "Right," she said. "You just loved him for his charming personality."

"I never said I loved him," I said. I hadn't, actually. I liked him well enough, but I'd never fallen in love with him. He'd never let me get that close. He didn't let anyone get to know him well, as far as I could see. We talked a lot, but it was rarely about anything personal. And it was rarely about anything that mattered. I wasn't looking for anything serious, so I didn't care all that much. And when he broke up with me, I was almost relieved. I wasn't sure why, though. I think I probably sensed that something was wrong. That something was missing from our relationship.

"Melissa," I said. "Tell me more about Hank's reaction. Was he desperate for the money? Is that why he was so angry?"

Melissa shrugged. "I don't think so," she said. "I never got the impression he was short of money. In fact, he seemed to have plenty. He was always buying me things—jewelry, clothes. And we went out to dinner at least twice a week. Always the best restaurants too.

Everything had to be the best with Hank. He wouldn't settle for anything less."

I shook my head and just thought for a while. That was just the opposite of the way he'd been with me. The only place he ever took me was BJ's or Barb and Artie's. He'd never bought me anything and he never took me out to dinner. I had never expected it. I just assumed he wasn't that kind of guy.

Something occurred to me. "Did he stop spending so much money after his father died?" I asked.

Melissa pursed her lips. "Just like a well run dry," she said. "That was one of the reasons I took up with Harry. I felt justified. I had a right to expect what I'd gotten used to."

I tried to keep my opinion of her from showing. I think I did a pretty good job. If she'd known how I felt, she probably would have stopped talking. "Did Harry know that?" I asked.

"Who knows?" Melissa said. "And for that matter, who cares? It's like Harry said, I was cheating on Hank and he knew he was carrying on with his father's girl. He's not so holy himself."

I certainly couldn't argue with that. I'd had so many questions in mind when I came to see Melissa, but I couldn't seem to remember any of them. I'd already learned more than I'd ever expected to. And I could always ask other questions later. I thanked Melissa for her time and told her I'd be in touch.

*   *   *

I called Dave as soon as I got home. "You wouldn't believe what happened at Melissa's," I said as soon as he answered the phone.

Dave snorted after I told him the story. "I had a feeling

about Harry," he said, "but I never would have guessed that. Do you think they could have done it together?"

I wrinkled my brow. "But why?" I said. "What motive could they have? Harry was the one with the money. If any one of the three of them had a motive for murder, it was Hank."

"Maybe he tried to kill one of them and they killed him in self-defense," Dave said.

"But then why would they put him in my basement?" I said. "Neither of them had ever heard of me."

"That's what they're claiming," Dave said. "How do you know they're not lying? Melissa could have found out about you. She could have put him there for revenge."

"It still doesn't seem right," I said. "If it really was self-defense, why would they need to cover it up?"

"Maybe they didn't think anyone would believe them," Dave said. "No one believes you, and you had nothing to do with it."

"Thanks for reminding me," I said. "By the way, do you still want to go and see Harry tomorrow night? He said he'd talk to me, but we didn't agree on a time."

"Let's wait," Dave said. "He's probably on his guard after tonight. Why don't we do some bar hopping instead? I'd like to talk to some of the guys Hank shot pool with."

"You know, I was surprised that BJ and Artie didn't come to the funeral," I said.

"Yeah, so was I," Dave said. "They weren't at the viewing either."

CHAPTER 7

I spent the next day looking through magazines and catalogs. I was trying to come up with some new craft ideas. I have a lot of items that are very popular. And because they're in high demand, I have to make a lot of them each year. But that can get boring. I was in the mood for a little change of pace.

I made an early dinner of biscuits and beef stew. I was having my second cup of tea when Dave came to my door. "Ready, Sherlock?" he said.

I laughed. "Ready as I'll ever be."

We went to Barb and Artie's first. It's only a few blocks from my house. I'd always found Artie easy to talk to. I figured we'd be better off starting with someone easy.

Artie gave me a big grin when I walked in. "Annie," he said, "it's been a long time. I've missed you." Then he wiped off the smile. "I was so sorry to hear about Hank. We all were."

I nodded with a sad face. "Yeah, I know," I said. "I was surprised I didn't see you at the funeral."

Artie looked away for a moment. Then he looked back at me. "I couldn't close the bar down," he said. "And I didn't have anyone to cover for me."

I was about to say something but I decided not to. I introduced Dave instead. Then I told him why we were there. Artie shook hands with Dave. But the smile he gave him was an uncomfortable one.

"Artie," I said. "Do you have any idea who could have killed Hank?"

Artie moved his hand across his face and through his hair. "Now how would I know that, Annie? What are you asking me that for?"

I gave him a kind smile. "I'm not asking because I think you did it," I said. As soon as I told him that, his face relaxed. "I was just hoping you might have heard something. Or seen something. Do you know of anyone who had it in for Hank?"

Artie gave me a crooked smile. "Now you know better than that," he said. "Everyone around here had it in for Hank. At least the ones who knew he was hustling them. I guess the others didn't mind so much. Of course, even they weren't too happy about losing money to him."

I nodded. "I know that, Artie. But did you ever hear any of those guys say something when we weren't around? Something to show they were really angry about it?"

Artie looked away again. He didn't answer right away. When he did, his face was a little pale. "You didn't hear this from me," he said. "Do you remember Mo Jackson?"

I frowned and shook my head. "The big red-headed guy," Artie said. "The one with the moustache. He always wears cowboy boots and a denim shirt."

I laughed and nodded. "Yeah, I know who you're talking about," I said. "But we hadn't seen him for a long time."

Artie paused for a moment. "Not since the last time he lost to Hank," he said. "He only came in on Tuesdays after that. You two never came in on Tuesdays. But he's been talking up a storm ever since. He tells everyone about Hank. Tells them what he looks like and not to play pool with him. Most folks thought he was just blowing off steam. But he was mighty angry, that's for sure."

"Does he know about Hank's murder?" I asked.

Artie frowned. "I don't know," he said. "I haven't seen him since then." When Artie saw Dave raise an eyebrow, he gave him a direct look. "Now that doesn't mean anything, son. He never did come in every week. Probably just a coincidence. Nothing more."

"Is there anything else you can think of to help us?" I asked Artie.

Artie picked up a dingy white cloth and started to wipe down the bar. "Nothing that comes to mind, little lady. Sorry I can't be more help."

"You've been a lot of help," I said. "We may be back, though. I think we'll try to catch Mo Jackson. And now that Hank's dead, I suppose any day will do."

Artie didn't answer. He just kept wiping the bar.

"Let's try BJ's," Dave said when we got outside. "Did you ever see this Mo guy there?"

I thought for a while. "I don't know," I said. "I never paid that much attention to him."

"What did you think of Artie's excuse for not being at the funeral?" Dave asked.

"Pretty flimsy," I said. "He could've found someone. He has three other bartenders."

"Were any of them at the funeral?" he said.

"No," I said. "But I wouldn't expect them to be. They knew us but they never really got friendly."

"But they knew about Hank's little hustling scam, didn't they?"

"Well, sure," I said. "They served him ginger ale too."

When we reached BJ's, the place was starting to get crowded. After six, things pick up quite a bit. BJ was there, as usual, and so was his female bartender. Her name is Amy. I always thought she had a crush on Hank. She was always giving him a come-on look whenever she handed him a drink. And I could tell she watched for us to come in. She never seemed to like me much.

"Hi, BJ. Hi, Amy," I said in a friendly voice. Amy forced a really fake smile and BJ looked a little nervous.

"Hi yourself, Annie," he said. "Who's your friend?"

I introduced both of them to Dave and explained what we were doing. Amy dropped her jaw and just stared. BJ scratched his head. "Do you think you can help us?" I said.

Amy closed her mouth and shrugged. "Like how?" she said. "I sure don't know anything about it. From what I heard they were blaming you. So how is it you're not in jail?"

I glared at her. "Because I didn't do it," I said.

"Then what was his body doing in your basement?" she asked. When I didn't answer her, BJ looked from one to the other of us and shook his head.

"Everyone knows about that," he said in a kindly voice. "The place has been buzzing ever since it happened. It's all anybody talks about anymore."

"Do they all think I did it?" I said.

BJ gave me a comforting smile. "No, honey. I'm sure they don't. They're just talking. That's all."

I sighed. I knew they were talking. And they were saying I did it. I hadn't realized it until then, but that really bothered me. I couldn't stand the idea that people thought I had actually killed someone.

"Do either of you know a guy named Mo Jackson?" I said. Amy and BJ looked at each other. Then they both looked across to the back room.

"He's here now," Amy said. "Playing pool."

"Thanks," Dave said as he grabbed my arm. "Come on. We're going to have a little talk with old Mo."

I tried to tell Dave on the way to the back room that Mo was at least six feet four. And he must have weighed more than two hundred and thirty pounds. Dave slowed down a bit when he saw him. But then he walked right up and held out his hand.

"I hear you're Mo Jackson," he said. "I'm Dave Barrio and I think you know Annie. She was Hank Samuels' girlfriend."

I could have strangled him right there. Mo sneered at me and let out a little growl. Then he pushed his way past Dave. "I got nothing to say to you," he said. "The man deserved what he got."

I raised my eyebrows and looked at Dave. It was a stupid thing for Mo to say under the circumstances. But it seemed unlikely he'd say it if he was guilty. I started to walk after him but Dave stopped me. "Let's talk to a few of these guys," he said. "They look a lot less hostile."

I looked around the room and realized that we were being watched. There were two guys playing at one table and one at another. I nodded in the direction of the man playing by himself. He was wearing tan slacks and a dark green crewneck sweater. He looked like he was close to forty years old. "Let's try him first," I said.

We walked over and introduced ourselves. Dave told him why we were there and asked if he could help us. The whole time we were talking, the man kept his eyes on the table. He sank one ball after another without missing a beat. When he'd cleared the table, he looked up.

"I don't know what I can tell you," he said in a calm voice. "Samuels wasn't well liked. He hustled people. But you probably know that. I think you're barking up the wrong tree, though. As far as I've heard, he never won enough off any one person to drive them to murder. It's a bit far-fetched, don't you think?"

"What about Mo?" Dave said. "We hear he was a little more upset than most."

The other man smiled. "Don't take Mo too seriously," he said. "He's a hothead. Always was. He means no harm. He just likes to talk. I've never seen him hurt a fly."

"Then why wouldn't he talk to us?" I said.

"You'll have to ask him that," the man said.

We found Mo at the bar, drinking a beer. I don't like to sit at bars anymore. It brings back bad memories from my drinking days. In fact, I don't like to be in bars at all. I used to try to tell Hank that but he wouldn't listen. He wasn't an alcoholic himself and he didn't care enough to try to understand. Dave understands and he's never been an alcoholic. The difference is, he really cares and he really listens.

I sat down next to Mo, and Dave sat on his other side. Mo looked at me and then Dave. He started to get up. "Don't go," I said in a kind voice. "We really don't mean to bother you. I'm being blamed for Hank's murder, and I'm just trying to prove that I didn't do it. I need all the help I can get."

Mo looked at me. "So you want to pin it on me. Is that it?"

"No, of course not," I said. Then I shrugged. "Unless you did it, of course."

Mo laughed. Then he laughed again as he shook his head. "Lady, I wish I could help you. I didn't kill him. And I don't know who did. Sure, I may have wanted to at times. But not really. Not real murder. I was just pissed off. You know what I mean? Real pissed off. But I had good reason."

I smiled at Mo. "Yeah, you did," I said. "I used to try to get him to stop hustling people but he wouldn't listen. I knew he'd get into trouble someday."

Mo frowned. "You don't really think one of the boys killed him, do you?"

I shrugged. "I don't know," I said. "I guess not. But I have to consider everything. I'm desperate. They really think I did it. His body was put in my basement."

"Yeah, so I heard. If it makes you feel any better, I never thought you did it. You don't look like the type."

I grinned so broadly that Mo couldn't help grinning back. Then I gave him a big hug. It took him by surprise but he accepted it nicely.

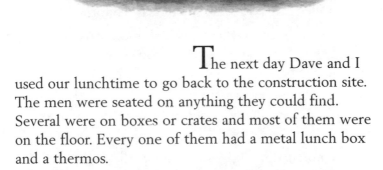

CHAPTER 8

The next day Dave and I used our lunchtime to go back to the construction site. The men were seated on anything they could find. Several were on boxes or crates and most of them were on the floor. Every one of them had a metal lunch box and a thermos.

Dave and I looked at each other. There were so many of them that we didn't know where to start. "I have an idea," Dave said. "Come on."

He walked toward the group and I followed. They were all chattering away and no one paid any attention to us. "Excuse me," Dave said in a loud voice. Three or four men turned to look at him but the others ignored him. I could see this wasn't going to be easy. Dave introduced us in the same loud voice. Then he told them why we were there. At that point, most of them stopped eating but no one spoke.

"Is there anyone here who overheard the argument between Hank Samuels and Fred Matthews the night before Matthews quit?" I said.

Still no response.

"Is there anyone here who knew Hank?" Dave asked.

The man closest to us said, "We all knew him. He worked with us."

"Did you know him well?" I said. "Did any of you become friends with him?"

A man way in the back of the group put up his hand to get our attention. "I knew Hank very well," he said. He got up and walked over to meet us. "I'm Joe Griffith," he said. "I heard a lot about you from Hank," he told me with a smile. "I'm very sorry about what happened."

"Could we go somewhere and talk more privately?" I said. "They're blaming me for his murder and I really need your help."

Joe took a deep breath. "Oh, my Lord," he said. He took my arm and started walking toward the main entrance where no one was sitting. "What can I do?" he said.

"How much time did you spend with Hank?" Dave asked.

"I went out for a drink with him after work almost every night of the week. We only stayed maybe half an hour. But it was a regular thing."

"Did he ever talk to you about anything personal?" I said.

Joe's face reddened a little. Then he coughed. "This is really important," Dave said. "I know there may be some things you feel funny talking about. But everything is important. Anything you can tell us may help Annie."

Joe looked at me. "I'm sorry," he said. "He did talk about

his personal life. And a lot of the talk was about you."

"And Melissa?" I said.

Joe raised an eyebrow. "And Melissa," he said. "I'm sorry."

I shrugged. "Don't feel sorry for me," I said. "I should have known better. There were plenty of signs. I guess I just didn't want to see them."

"I know this is uncomfortable for you," Dave said, "but could you tell us exactly what he said?"

Joe let out a big sigh. Then he looked at me. "Are you okay with that?" he said.

I nodded. "Sure. Go ahead. None of that matters now anyway. We broke up a month before he was killed."

"I know," Joe said. "That was one of the things we talked about." Joe paused for a moment before he continued. "Hank had been having an affair with Melissa for something like five years. But every once in a while, he felt like he needed a little variety." Joe looked at me and winced.

I smiled. "It's okay," I said. "Please just tell us anything you can. Right now my entire life is at stake. That's a lot more important than hurt feelings."

"Okay," Joe said. "I see your point." He looked down at the floor. "Hank had at least two or three others, besides you, while he was seeing Melissa," he said. "I'm not sure I could even remember their names, though. There was a pretty big gap between you and the one before you."

For some reason, that made me feel good. Ridiculous, but true. "How long of a gap?" Dave said.

"At least a year," Joe said. "But the thing he'd been talking about lately was Sharon, his wife. He met her when they were in junior high school. She was his first girlfriend. They got married when they were eighteen because she was pregnant with Harry."

"He told me that he broke up with Annie because he wanted to try to make his marriage work," Dave said. "Is that what he told you?"

Joe nodded. "Strange as it may seem, that's what he said."

"Did you believe him?" I said.

"Not at first," Joe said. "I just assumed he was joking. It just didn't fit with his character. You know what I mean?"

I nodded. "What made you change your mind?" I said.

"I think the thing that really convinced me was his breaking up with Melissa too. He'd always broken up with the other ones after a few months, but he'd always stuck with Melissa. He stayed with you longer than most," he added with a kind smile.

I smiled back. "Thanks," I said. "Did any of these women ever find out he was married?"

Joe made a face. "They usually had it figured out after about two months. He could fool them for a while but they always caught on."

I blushed and Joe gave me an uncomfortable look. "Sorry," he said again. "If it makes you feel any better, Melissa never knew either. Or if she did, she never said anything to Hank."

"In five whole years, she never guessed he was married?" Dave said. "I find that a little hard to believe."

"Yeah, I know what you mean," Joe said.

"Why did he suddenly want to make his marriage work?" I said. "Why after all that time? Did he still think he loved her?"

Joe gave me a funny look. "I know women find this hard to believe. They think if we're cheating on them that we can't possibly love them. But we can."

I looked at Dave and he looked at the floor. Then I looked back at Joe. "That doesn't make sense to me and I don't buy it," I said.

Joe shrugged. "Women never do," he said. "But the fact is, Hank said he loved her and wanted to try to make it work again. You have to understand something about Hank. He grew up thinking he'd be taken care of all his life. He assumed his old man would leave him the family business. He was the only boy. Not that that matters," he quickly added when he saw my face. "But his sister didn't want it and Hank always knew that. He never planned ahead. Never set aside anything for the future. When his dad left the business to Harry, his whole life fell apart. That was only a few weeks before he met you," he said to me.

"He never said a word about it," I said.

"I think he was too ashamed," Joe said. "He seemed to have lost all his self-esteem after that. He felt like a failure. He had nothing left. Before that, he'd acted like he was on top of the world. Then everything changed. I think he wanted to make just one thing go right. The only thing he had left to work on was his marriage. I really believe that's why he broke up with you."

I sighed and thought for a few moments. "Do you know if it was working at all?"

Joe shrugged. "It was too soon to tell," he said, "but he did seem happier. And I know they started spending time together. They had Marge and me over for supper one night."

"When was that?" Dave said.

"Less than a week before he died," Joe said. Then he looked away for a moment and closed his eyes.

I gave him a few moments before I asked my next

question. "Did you ever meet Melissa or any of the other women?" I said then.

Joe shook his head. "No, I didn't. The only time I spent with Hank, except for the night we were at his house, was after work at the bar. I'd never even met his wife until that night."

"Do you think his wife knew about Melissa and the rest of us?" I asked in a small voice.

Joe looked at me and opened his palm. "She must have," he said. "But she may have convinced herself she was wrong. Sometimes it's easier not to know the truth. Do you know what I mean?"

I nodded and looked away.

"Do you think his wife could have killed him?" Dave asked. "Or how about Melissa?"

"Either of them could have, I suppose. But I have no reason to suspect them. As far as Hank knew, they didn't know about each other. There wouldn't be any motive, especially for his wife. Why would she kill him when he was trying to fix their marriage? She would have been happier with him than ever."

"Not if he came clean about Annie and the others," Dave said. "He could have felt he had to get it off his conscience. And if he did that, she'd have every reason to hate him."

Joe raised his eyebrows. "Well, if he did tell her, he never told me about it," he said.

We asked Joe a few more questions but didn't learn anything useful. We thanked him for his time and I told him we'd be in touch if we found anything out.

CHAPTER
9

As we were about to get into Dave's car, Paul ran toward us. We hadn't seen him inside. "Have you made any progress yet?" he asked me. "Were you talking to Jeff again?"

"No, we came to talk to the rest of the guys," I said. "Joe Griffith said he and Hank were pretty good friends. He knew a lot about his personal life."

Paul frowned. "I didn't know they were such good friends," he said. "Hank did mention Joe from time to time. I thought they just knew each other at work."

"Well, Joe knew about Hank's wife and all of his girlfriends so they obviously talked a lot. And he knew Hank left me and Melissa because he wanted to make his marriage work."

Paul didn't know who Melissa was either, so I let Dave explain. "What about Jeff?" Paul said after Dave was finished. "Did he answer any of your questions?"

"Yeah, he was pretty helpful," I said. "He said he'd overheard Hank and some guy named Fred Matthews arguing one night."

Paul's face clouded over and he stared at me for a few moments. "Fred Matthews?" he said.

"Yeah, why? Do you know him?"

"Everyone knows him," Paul said. "Or at least they know who he is. He's been missing for almost two months."

I shook my head. "I don't think he's missing," I said. "Jeff told us he quit the day after the argument between him and Hank. He called in and gave him his notice."

Paul's jaw dropped. "That doesn't make any sense," he said. "He has a wife and two kids. They reported him missing. She says he left for work one morning and never came home again. She was at the site asking us about him."

"What do they think happened to him?" I said.

Paul shook his head. "I don't know," he said. "The police were here questioning everyone. But we never heard anything. To be honest with you, we all assumed he just took off for other parts. Like maybe he wanted to get away from his wife and kids. I know that sounds harsh but it happens more often than you think."

"Yeah, you may be right," I said with a sigh.

We said good-bye to Paul and drove to McDonald's again because Dave won't eat anywhere else.

"What does handsome Harry do during the day? Do you know?" Dave asked me with a mouth full of french fries.

"I have no idea," I said. "But my guess would be that he probably spends some time overseeing his cement business."

"Why don't we stop by and pay him a little surprise visit?" he said. "Do you know where it is?"

"No. At least not for sure. Melissa didn't tell me what it was called. But I'd be willing to bet that it's Samuels' Cement behind the old warehouse."

Dave laughed and wolfed down a pie. "Let's go," he said. "If he's not there, maybe someone will tell us where we can find him."

We were only five minutes away, and it was just a little after two-thirty. When we arrived, we saw three spotlessly clean cement mixers lined up in a row. Each one had "Samuels' Cement" printed on the side in bright yellow letters. There was plenty of room for others that probably were out at job sites. The whole place looked neat and well managed. We parked in a gravel lot filled with cars and pickups and walked around a bit before we went inside. We saw at least ten men working and three of them appeared to be supervisors. No sign of Harry, though.

We walked inside and looked around for an office. Across a large space that looked like the inside of a warehouse, we saw a partially opened door. As we came near, I heard voices and I grabbed Dave's arm. I motioned for him to walk along the wall with me. I was in the mood for a little spying.

The first voice I heard was not Harry's. I couldn't quite place it at first. But eventually I realized that it was Hank's wife. I'd only heard her speak when I met her at the viewing, but she has a very unusual voice. A little like Katharine Hepburn's, believe it or not.

"I want what I'm entitled to," she was saying in a cold voice. "You know I can't survive on my own without your father. We counted on this business all our lives. It was our only plan for the future. We expected to retire on it.

You know your father never saved a dime."

"Ma, I've heard this a thousand times before," Harry replied. "What do you want from me? I didn't ask to be given this business. It was as much a surprise to me as it was to you and Dad."

"I don't believe that," she said with a slight hiss. "I think you did know. You must have been told. Your grandfather never would have entrusted the business to you unless he was sure you wanted it. And unless he was sure you'd do a good job running it."

There was silence for several moments. "What do you want, Ma?" Harry finally said.

"I want an income," she said. "And I want a good one. I'm entitled to that. I've worked hard all my life. I made a home for you and your father. And now I have nothing."

I heard a drawer open and close. After a few more moments of silence, I heard Harry say, "Will this do for now?"

After a slight pause, his mother muttered, "Yes." Then Dave and I quickly moved behind some boxes when we heard movement inside. Mrs. Samuels slammed the door behind her and walked toward the exit with hurried footsteps. Harry remained inside. We waited about three minutes before we knocked on the door.

"Come in," Harry said in a gruff voice.

When he saw who it was, his already sober look turned to annoyance and discomfort.

"What do you want?" he said. "I'm busy."

"I'm sorry," I said in as kind a voice as I could. "But you said you wanted to help us find your father's murderer. That's why we're here."

Harry pursed his lips and slowly put down his pen.

Then he glared at Dave and me. "And just how do you think I can help?" he said.

I sighed and sat down on a clean brown metal chair. "Tell us anything you can," I said. "Do you think your dad was in any sort of trouble?"

Harry frowned. "What's that supposed to mean?" he said.

"We don't know," Dave said. "What Annie means is, do you think someone was giving him a hard time about something? Could he have owed someone money? Was he in financial trouble? Anything. Just tell us anything you can think of."

Harry paused for a few moments before he spoke. "I know he was in financial trouble for a while. But the last couple of months before his death he was spending money like crazy. He said he got a few raises at work."

I nodded. "He told me about the raises too," I said. "We just talked to his boss the other day and he admitted he'd given him the raises. He said he was a very good worker and he always rewards his men for good work."

Harry shrugged. "That's not so hard to believe," he said. "I reward my employees the same way. If you don't keep them happy, they go somewhere else. And it's hard to find good men these days."

"Okay," I said. "What else can you tell us? Did you see your father much?"

Harry sucked in his cheeks. "Not since I inherited this business," he said.

I gave him a sympathetic smile. "Was he really angry with you?"

"He hated me," Harry said.

"I doubt that," I said. "I can understand his being

disappointed. But I can't believe he hated you. You're his son."

Harry laughed and it sounded pretty bitter. "He and my mom had me over to dinner every Sunday night for my entire adult life. When my grandfather died, I was no longer welcome."

Dave shook his head. "Sorry to hear that," he said. "You're right. That was pretty unfair. Did you know you were going to inherit the business before it happened?" Dave asked.

Harry stiffened a little but calmed down right away. Then he looked across the room. "Yeah, I knew," he said without looking at us. "My grandfather told me about a year before he died. He had cancer and they gave him a year to live. He didn't quite make it. Nine months was all he got."

"I'm sorry," I said.

Harry shrugged. "I tried to talk my grandfather out of it at first. I knew my dad was counting on it. He talked about it all our lives. It's easy to say now that he should have planned ahead. But who can blame him? How many people would if they were sure they'd inherit a fortune before they reached retirement age?"

"I hear you," Dave said. "You didn't tell your dad about it until it happened?"

"No," Harry said. "I knew what was coming. I wasn't in any hurry to experience it."

"I can understand that," Dave said. "Is it hard to run this place? It must take a lot of work."

Harry nodded. But the look on his face was a proud one. "It does take a lot of work," he said. "I didn't know the first thing about the cement business until my grandfather gave me the news. But he taught me everything he could in the nine months he had left. I don't know what I would've done if he hadn't."

"Did your dad know anything about the cement business?" I said. "Do you think he'd have known how to run it?"

Harry sighed. "That was the saddest part of this whole thing," he said. "My dad knew everything, and I mean everything, about this business. He learned it from the ground up. He was here with my grandfather from the time he could walk. My grandfather was training him for the business. He'd always intended to give it to him. I think that's one of the reasons my dad was so angry. As far as I know, my grandfather never told him he wasn't getting it."

"Do you know what made your grandfather change his mind?" Dave said.

"Drugs," Harry said. "My dad was really heavy into drugs for a long time and my grandfather could never forgive him. He never trusted him after that."

"When was this?" I said. "He never used drugs when he was around me. He never even talked about them."

"It wasn't something my dad was proud of," Harry said. "He spent two years in a rehab unit. But that was over fifteen years ago. He's been clean ever since. I tried to tell my grandfather that. I thought he should have been proud of him for getting himself out from under all of that. It was a long haul. He worked damn hard at it, and he had no one who really understood. I was too young to know better, I guess. My mom just couldn't understand. She thought he was weak. She just couldn't see that it was an illness." Harry shook his head. "He must have told her a thousand times that beating it showed how strong he really was. But she'd insist that if he was strong, he wouldn't have started in the first place."

I gave Harry an understanding look and so did Dave. "I hear what you're saying," Dave said. "I've been there."

Harry raised his eyebrows at Dave and then gave him a grateful smile. "Thanks, man," he said. "It's nice to know there's someone out there who can relate."

We talked a few minutes longer and then decided it was time to go. I wanted to leave when we were on friendly terms.

CHAPTER 10

"Do you think he did it?" Dave asked after we got in the car.

"Who? Harry?" I said. "No way. Why would he do it? He obviously loved his father. Besides, what motive could he possibly have?"

"I don't know," Dave said. "I'm still working on that."

After Dave dropped me at home, I decided to look up Martha Samuels (now called Martha Richards) in the phone book. According to the obituary, Martha was Hank's sister. She might know something helpful about Hank.

I called Martha. I'd never met her and I assumed that she didn't know I existed. I was wrong.

"I know all about you," she told me after I introduced myself. Her tone of voice wasn't very friendly but it wasn't entirely hostile, either. "Hank talked about you a lot."

I'll have to admit that made me feel pretty good. It was nice to know he considered me important enough to mention. I really wanted to ask her about it but I held myself back for the time being. Instead, I told her about my being suspected in Hank's murder.

"Would you be willing to talk to me?" I asked her.

She hesitated for a moment. "Sure," she said. "I'll talk to you. I want his killer found as much as you do. What did you have in mind?"

"Anything you want," I said. "I can come to your house or we can meet somewhere. You choose the time."

"Why don't you come here?" she said. "I'll be home all night and I'm not doing anything. Stop by anytime. I'm at 622 Woodbine, apartment 7."

I told her I'd try to make it around seven o'clock, and then I called Dave. "You want to come with me?" I asked him.

"Sorry," he said. "I'm going out with Marla. But call me tonight and let me know what happens."

I was disappointed for more than one reason, but I tried not to let it show. "Sure," I said. "I'll call you at ten. Is that too early?"

He laughed. "Afraid so, kiddo. Make it tomorrow morning, now that I think about it."

Me and my big mouth. "Okay," I said and hung up.

I know this sounds really stupid, but every time Dave goes out with someone, I get jealous. We've never been anything more than friends so it doesn't make sense. But I still feel that way, every time.

I did some paperwork for the next hour. Then I worked on a wooden birdhouse I was making until it was time to go.

Martha lived on the first floor of a two-story building with dingy walls and crying babies all over the place. Most of the doors were open a crack. The smells of a number of different meals mingled together with other odors I'd rather not describe. The effect was kind of sickening.

Martha's door was closed. I knocked three times before she answered it. When she saw me, she gave me a startled look. I gave her a curious one back and she laughed. "Sorry," she said. "It's just that you look so young. A lot younger than Hank."

I smiled. "I am younger than he was, but I'm a lot older than I look," I said.

Martha was almost six feet tall with stringy, dark blond hair. Her clothes were wrinkled and old. She was smoking a cigarette and holding some sort of alcoholic drink with the same hand. "Sit anywhere you like," she said as she blew a ring of smoke.

I chose the cleanest looking chair I could find and sat on the very edge of it. I couldn't help wondering how the daughter of a wealthy cement businessman could end up living in such conditions. The man not only denied Hank his promised inheritance. He obviously ignored his daughter too.

When I sat down, Martha gave me an amused look. "You didn't know about Hank's wife, did you?" she said. It was more of a statement than a question.

I shook my head. "I didn't know about Melissa either."

Martha laughed and almost choked on her drink. "Then you probably don't know about Amy or Lila, huh?"

I winced and she laughed again. I was starting to get irritated. I didn't think it was all that funny. Then something occurred to me. "Amy isn't a bartender, is she?"

"Yeah, do you know her?"

I let out a big sigh. "I think I do," I said. "Does she work at BJ's Tap?"

Martha shrugged. "I don't know," she said. "All I know is she's from one of the places where Hank played pool."

I tightened my jaw. If Hank weren't already dead, I think I would've killed him myself. Martha saw the look on my face and wrinkled her forehead. "What did you see in my brother, anyway?" she asked.

I opened my mouth and closed it again. The truth was, I wasn't sure. But I didn't want to tell her that. I think she read my mind. She smiled and said, "So what can I do for you?"

"Tell me anything you can," I said. "I need to prove I didn't do it. I'm trying to find out what was going on in his life. It might help me figure out what happened. First of all, who's Lila? Do you have any idea where I can find her?"

"Sorry," Martha said. "I have no idea at all."

I sighed. "Did Hank ever tell you he was in any kind of trouble?" I asked.

Martha glanced at me sideways and took another sip of her drink. "What kind of trouble you talking about?" she said.

"Anything," I said. "Financial trouble. Trouble at work. Was he afraid of anyone? Just anything."

She looked across the room and started playing with the fringe on a pillow. But she didn't give me an answer. "Please," I said, "you have no reason to protect him from anything now. He's dead. No one can hurt him. But I could end up in prison for the rest of my life and I didn't do anything."

She took a long drag on her cigarette and another slow drink. "I don't know what to tell you," she said without looking at me. "He did come into a lot of money all of a sudden. But he wouldn't talk about it much. All he said was his ship finally came in. He didn't act like he was in any kind of trouble, though. Fact is, he seemed happier than ever. It was like he was walking on a cloud."

"He didn't give you any idea where it came from?" I said.

Martha shook her head. "Not a one," she said.

"Didn't he tell you about the raises he got at work?" I asked.

Martha wrinkled her brow. "Raises?" she said in a loud voice. "There ain't no way he would have gotten any raises. He was lucky to have that job. He was always getting told he'd get fired if he didn't start showing up on time. He never got no raises."

I stared at her with my mouth open. "When did he tell you that?" I said. "It couldn't have been recently."

Martha shrugged. "I don't remember when he said it. All I know is his boss was pretty pissed off with him for coming in late all the time."

I nodded and let it drop. I'd already talked to Jeff Rogers. He'd admitted giving Hank the raises so I knew it was true. What I was wondering was if Martha had some reason to want me to believe that it wasn't true. And there was another possibility. Hank might have goofed off for a while. But then he might have started to take the threats of being fired seriously and cleaned up his act. Jeff may have given him the raises to encourage his good behavior. I decided to have a talk with Paul about it. He was as close to Hank as anyone, and he worked with him every day.

I moved on to the topic that interested me the most. "What did Hank say about me?" I said.

Martha looked at me with pity and shook her head. "It was all good, honey. That's all I can say. I don't remember no particulars."

I sighed and turned down my mouth. "Sorry," she said. "He liked you a lot. A lot more than the rest."

"What about the others?" I said. "Do you think any of them could have killed him?"

"Sure, why not? He was cheating on every one of you, and none of you knew he was married. Someone finds out that kind of thing, it can make them plenty mad. It would make me mad, I can tell you."

"What did he tell you about Amy?" I asked. "When did he start up with her?"

"She was a new one," Martha said. "He didn't pick up with her until a few weeks before he died."

I smiled and Martha gave me a weird look. "So it wasn't until after we broke up," I said.

Martha nodded. "That's right, hon. He didn't throw you over for her, if that's what you're worried about."

I laughed. "I was," I said. "It seems silly to think about that now but I can't help it." Then I frowned. "Wait a minute," I said. "He told at least two people that he broke up with me and Melissa because he wanted to try to make his marriage work."

Martha burst out laughing. "His marriage!" she said. "There ain't no way he would have done that. He was through with Sharon over ten years ago. He never would have gone back to that. They may have lived in the same house together but there was no marriage there."

"Then why did he stay with her?" I said.

Martha shrugged. "I used to ask him the same thing. He never gave me a straight answer. The only reason I could ever come up with was Sharon's mother. She's in her late eighties and she has quite a bit of money. I figure Hank thought it made Sharon worth staying with."

This was getting weirder by the minute. "Can you tell me anything else?" I said. "Anything you can think of."

Martha shook her head. "I can't think of a thing, honey. I'm sorry I can't help you. If it makes you feel any better, I do feel awful sorry for you."

I gave her a grateful smile. "Thanks," I said. "It does help. Lately, I've been feeling like everyone thinks I'm guilty."

We talked a bit more and Martha agreed to let me see her again if I came up with any more questions. As soon as I got home, I picked up the phone to call Dave. Then I remembered Marla, and I put the phone down. Then I thought even more about Marla and picked it up again. Dave answered on the fifth ring. His voice was a little groggy. I told him what Martha had said without even mentioning Marla. He didn't mention her either.

"How would you like to come with me during lunch tomorrow?" I said. "I want to talk to Paul about all of this."

"That's a good idea," he said. "But maybe we should call him and ask him to meet us somewhere. It might be better to talk where we know we won't be overheard."

I agreed and said I'd call Paul as soon as we hung up.

"What's so mysterious?" Paul asked when I gave him my request.

"It's nothing big," I said. "We just want to ask you

some questions about Hank's job, but we don't want anyone to hear."

"Okay," Paul said. But he sounded wary. "Let's meet at Samson's. I can be there by ten after twelve. And it's far enough away that none of the guys is likely to be there."

After I said good-bye to Paul, I made myself some vegetable soup with Italian bread. Then I got out a notebook and started writing while I ate. I hadn't kept any notes on the interviews we'd had. That was a mistake. I could remember pretty well what everyone had said, but it was a struggle. I decided right then and there that I'd take notes after every interview from then on.

CHAPTER 11

I got up early the next day and worked for almost two hours before I ate breakfast. At ten o'clock I went through my notes over my second cup of tea. I was dying to talk to Amy. I was dying to strangle her, to tell you the truth. I couldn't stand it. I had to see her. I put away my paints and drove to BJ's.

Amy and BJ were there, taking care of the early regulars. I'd been there in the morning only once. It was a day that Hank planned to hustle a guy he'd heard came in early. He'd also heard he had a lot of money. I was glad to see he wasn't there that day.

I walked over to the bar and sat down. Amy was washing glasses. She looked up, saw who I was, and looked down again. "Amy," I said. "I think we need to talk."

She kept right on washing. "What about?" she muttered.

"You and Hank," I said. Then I just waited. She rinsed three glasses before she looked up. She narrowed her eyes and gave me a dirty look.

"I don't know what you mean," she said.

"I think you do," I answered. "Hank's sister knows all about you and Hank. She said you started seeing each other only a few weeks before he died."

"So what do you care?" she said in a teenage sort of way. "He'd already broken up with you."

I took a deep breath. "Were you still seeing him when he died?" I asked.

She pursed her lips. "Yes," she said, "if it's any of your business. And I didn't kill him, if that's what you're getting at. We had a really good relationship. He really cared about me."

I tried to keep a neutral expression. "How long were you going out?" I said as if I couldn't quite remember.

"Three and a half weeks," she said. "And every minute was wonderful."

Yeah, I'll bet. The conversation wasn't really getting me anywhere. I decided to try something new. "Amy," I said. "They're planning to charge me with his murder. And I'm sure you know I didn't do it. I know we've never been friends but I need your help. I don't hold it against you for going out with Hank. I hope you don't hold it against me."

She shrugged and her face softened a little. "So what do you want?" she said.

"I just need to find out if anything unusual was going on before he died. Did he talk to you about anything that was bothering him?"

Amy wrinkled her brow. "Not that I can think of,"

she said. Then she smiled. "We didn't do a whole lot of talking, if you know what I mean."

I did and I got the urge to strangle her again. But I remained perfectly calm. "Did he seem like he was worried about anything?" I said. "Or was he afraid of anybody?"

She frowned again. "I don't think so," she said. "Unless you mean like his job or something."

My eyes opened wide. "He was worried about his job?" I said. "What did he say?"

Amy shook her head. "I didn't say he was worried about his job," she said. "But he didn't like it very much. He was talking about quitting."

"Did he say why?" I asked.

"No," Amy said, "but I think it was because he didn't need it anymore. He didn't need the money."

I looked at her in surprise. "Why not?" I said. "Where was he getting money other than from his job?"

"I don't know where he was getting it," she said. "But he was getting it from somewhere. He was loaded."

I was more confused than I'd been before I came. I looked at my watch. It was a little after eleven and Dave was meeting me at the house at eleven-thirty. I said good-bye to Amy and went home. I took out my notebook as soon as I got there and wrote down everything Amy had told me. Then I wrote down some ideas that had come to me on the drive home.

When I shared them with Dave fifteen minutes later, he agreed with me. "Let's go see Paul," he said. "Maybe we can straighten some of this out."

We arrived at Samson's at ten after twelve. Paul was already waiting for us in one of the large booths. He gave us a slightly nervous look when he saw us come in. We sat down across from him, and he and Dave shook hands. A waitress came over right away and asked what we wanted. After we ordered, Paul started playing with his silverware.

"Is something bothering you?" I asked him with a frown.

Paul quickly put down the spoon. "No. I just want to know what this is all about. Why the secret meeting? What's going on?"

"Nothing's going on," I said to Paul. "We just want to ask you a few questions that involve Hank's work. I didn't want anyone else to hear."

"Why? Do you suspect one of the men?" he asked.

I shrugged. "I don't suspect anyone in particular," I said. "But you have to realize that everyone's a possible suspect."

"Including you," Paul said. I was surprised by the remark. I was also surprised by the resentful look on his face.

"Yes, including me," I said. "Paul, I hope you don't think we suspect you. It's just that you knew Hank better than most of the guys, and I know you too. I'd much rather talk to you than someone I don't trust."

Paul's face relaxed and he smiled. "Sorry," he said. "Go ahead. What's on your mind?"

Dave told him the story about Hank's raises. Paul looked from Dave to me and back again. "That's impossible," he said. "Rogers and Hank couldn't stand each other. That's why I was so surprised when Rogers was willing to talk to you."

"Did he give regular raises?" Dave said. "For instance, did he give everyone a raise after they'd been there a certain length of time?"

Paul nodded. "Everyone gets a two percent increase after the first year. Then we get another two percent every six months."

"So why would he leave Hank out," Dave said, "even if he didn't like him?"

"He wouldn't," Paul said. "But from the sound of it, he was giving Hank a lot more than the standard raises."

Dave nodded. "So it seems."

Something suddenly occurred to me. "When was the last raise you received?" I asked Paul.

"The first week of January," he said. "We get one at the beginning of the year and another one in June."

I was frowning and they were both looking at me. "What's the matter?" Paul said.

"Hank got the first of the raises he told me about on March 18th," I said. "I remember it because he said we should go out and celebrate St. Patrick's Day. And I told him he was a day too late, and neither of us was Irish. He wanted to go out because he just got a raise, and he wanted to celebrate."

Paul was shaking his head. "I don't get it," he said. "I can't see Rogers giving Hank extra raises."

"Rogers told us he gave him the raises," I said.

"He probably thought you were talking about the standard ones," Paul said. "Did you mention when he got them?"

I thought for a moment. "No, I don't think so," I said. "It never occurred to me."

Paul nodded. "I'm sure he assumed you were talking about the ones he gives everyone."

"Then Hank must have been lying about where the extra money came from," Dave said.

"I know," I said. "And I have an idea where he might have gotten it."

"Where?" Dave and Paul both said at once.

"I'll tell you when I'm sure," I said. I quickly wrote down my phone number and address for Paul and said, "Call me if you think of anything else."

We left Paul at the restaurant and Dave took me home. "We need to go and see Harry again," I said. "And also his mother."

Dave widened his eyes. "You want to talk to Hank's wife?" he said. "How are you going to explain who you are?"

"I don't know," I said, "but I'll come up with something."

When I got in the house, I called Harry and asked if we could see him again. He agreed without too much hesitation to meet at one-thirty the next day. Then I asked him for his mother's phone number. He wasn't as quick to agree to that. When I assured him that I had no intention of telling her about me and Hank, he gave in.

Then I called Sharon Samuels. I was almost hoping I wouldn't reach her. But she answered on the first ring.

I fumbled my way through an introduction. I told her I was a secretary for the construction company. I also told her that Hank's body was put in my basement and that I had no idea why. She actually invited me to come and see her. I didn't even have to ask. She didn't give me much time either. She suggested I come right over. I was about to ask if I could bring Dave, but I decided against it. I had a strong suspicion she would say no.

When I pulled up in front of Sharon's house, I just sat and looked for a while. I had never seen it before.

Hank had never taken me home with him. The reason was obvious now, but I'd always wondered why.

The house had blue aluminum siding and a brown door. The yard was small and made of gravel. I rang the bell and tried to calm myself down. I hadn't expected to be so nervous, and I didn't know how to deal with it. When she answered the door, Sharon gave me a cold look. When she asked me to come in, her voice was just as cold. She knew. I could just feel it.

I followed her into the living room. She sat in a chair and motioned for me to take the couch. Then she looked me straight in the eye. "You had an affair with Hank," she said in an even tone.

I felt the blood rush to my face. "I'll bet you're wondering how I know," she said.

I stared at her and started to stammer. "Hank told me," she said. "He told me about all of them."

"When did he tell you?" I said.

She shrugged. "He told me about you about a month ago."

"How about Melissa?" I asked.

"I've known about her for years," Sharon said. "Melissa was his standby," she added with an odd smile.

I frowned at her. "Why in the world did you stay with him if you knew all that?" I said.

She shrugged. "Where else would I go? I married Hank when I was eighteen. I have never worked a day in my life. He was kind to me."

She stopped when I gave her a funny look. "You have to understand something," she said. "The spark went out of our marriage a few years after Harry was born. Hank was never home. He never gave me any help with the baby. And we never spent any time together.

But we didn't argue or fight. We just stopped caring for each other."

I was having a hard time trying to imagine such a life. I think it showed on my face. "None of that's important now," she said. "I asked you here because I wanted to see what you look like."

I blushed again and she smiled. "I can't help but be curious," she said. "You'd want to know too."

I wasn't sure I would, and I was feeling very uncomfortable. I squirmed in my seat.

"What can I do for you?" Sharon said in a kind voice.

I gave her a grateful smile. "Do you know if Hank was in any kind of trouble? Or was he afraid of anyone?"

She shook her head. "No, not that he told me. You have to realize, we didn't share much of our daily lives."

I nodded. "Do you have any idea where he got all that money?"

Sharon's face flushed and she wrinkled her brow. "What money?" she asked quietly.

I stared at her for a few moments not knowing what to say. Then I told her the story Hank had told me.

CHAPTER
12

Dave and I arrived at Harry's office at exactly one-thirty the next day. As soon as we sat down, I gave Harry a direct look.

"Harry," I said, "I know you told us that you hadn't seen your father since you inherited the business. And I'm not accusing you of lying. What I'd like to know is if you saw him at all."

Harry frowned. "Of course I did. And I talked to him too. What's the point of this?"

"Had you been giving your father money?" I asked.

Harry hesitated a moment. "I did from time to time," he said. "After my grandfather died, I sent my dad a few checks. I felt guilty. I knew he was hurting. I was trying to make up for it somehow. I wanted to do what I could to help out."

"So then it was from you that he was getting all that money?" Dave said.

"All what money?" Harry asked.

"You told us yourself that he was spending money like crazy the last couple of months before he died. Did you give him that money?"

"No," Harry said with an irritated look. "If I had, I would have told you that to begin with."

"Did he take the money you gave him?" Dave asked.

Harry laughed. "You better believe he took it. He wanted more than I was willing to part with. He believed it was all his, you have to understand. He didn't think I was being generous. He just thought I was giving him a very small part of what he deserved."

I suddenly remembered the conversation we'd overheard between Harry and his mother. "How did your mother feel?" I said. "Did she have the same attitude?"

"She still does," Harry said. "She expects me to support her for the rest of her life."

"Does she need the money that badly?" I asked.

Harry raised his eyebrows. "Well, she could use a little help now and then. But she stands to inherit a lot from my grandmother. She's already in her eighties and my mom's an only child. She won't need any help then."

"How often was your dad pressuring you for money?" Dave said. "And how hard?"

Harry gave Dave a dirty look. "Too often," he said. "But I didn't kill him to get him off my back. Is that what you're implying?"

Dave shrugged. "We have to cover all the bases," he said. "Don't take it personally."

Harry sneered at Dave and then looked at me. "Is there anything else?" he asked me in a weary voice. "If not, I really need to get back to work."

I gave him a warm smile. "Nothing for now. Thanks, Harry. We'll be in touch."

When we got back to the car, Dave slumped down in his seat and groaned.

"What's the matter?" I said.

"I don't know," he said. "Just when I think we're getting somewhere, I find out we're barking up the wrong tree. What do you think? Do you believe what Harry said?"

"Yeah, I really do," I said. "We overheard him talking to his mother, remember? He isn't an easy touch. I don't know why he would have been any easier with Hank."

"Except that Hank was the one who was supposed to get the business," Dave said. "His mother was just along for the ride."

"Well, that's true," I said. "But I still don't think he killed his father just because he was asking for money."

After Dave dropped me at home, I got out my writing pad and made my usual notes about our meeting with Harry. Then I started going through the rest of my notes. When I was finished, I was as confused as ever. As far as I could see, almost everyone involved made a pretty decent suspect.

Melissa could have been furious for more than one reason. First, Hank "lost" the fortune he'd told her he would inherit, and he stopped treating her like a queen. Then to top it off, he broke up with her after five long years. She may have found out about me too. People have been known to kill for a lot less than that.

Then there was Amy. Maybe he didn't treat her quite as nicely as she'd led me to believe. He may have dumped her too. Or he could have cheated on her already and she couldn't take it. She never had liked me. She might have decided to frame me to get back at me. And Lila was another possibility, whoever she was.

Sharon Samuels was my prime suspect, though. She'd known all those years that Hank was cheating on her. Or so she said. Maybe she really hadn't known. Maybe she really didn't find out until he told her a month or so before he died. She could have framed me too, because I'd been going out with him. She had no way of knowing I hadn't known about her.

Of course, there were all those pool players—all the men Hank had hustled and gotten money from. Even those who hadn't known he was a hustler had probably found out from Mo Jackson. Artie said he'd been telling everyone about Hank. He started telling them shortly before Hank was killed. I couldn't forget Artie or BJ either. They weren't exactly fond of Hank.

Martha didn't have a motive as far as I could see. But I still wasn't positive about Harry. He was a possibility. I couldn't deny it.

As I mulled it over, there was one thing I couldn't get off my mind: the money Hank had suddenly come into. Hank may have lied to me about where it came from. He told Martha about the money. But she said he never mentioned a raise. And she was sure it couldn't have been a raise. Hank had told her that he was in danger of being fired.

I decided to call Jeff Rogers. I would have stopped to see him in person, but I didn't feel like wasting the time. He was there but I had to wait about five minutes. I didn't tell the woman who answered who I was. I was afraid he wouldn't take the call if he knew. When he finally came to the phone, he sounded hurried.

"Rogers here," he barked into the phone. I told him who I was and he groaned.

"I just have a quick question," I said. "Did you give Hank a raise on March 18th? Or did you only give him the standard raises you gave everyone else?"

Jeff didn't answer for what seemed like minutes. When he did speak, his voice was full of anger. "My business dealings with my men are none of your business," he said. "I've already explained this to you. I don't want to hear from you again." And he hung up.

I sat for a while with a frown on my face. Then I made a note about our conversation.

I tried for several minutes to come up with a way to find out the truth. No one but Hank and Jeff could really know when and if Jeff gave him the raises. And I had no way of getting to Jeff's records. Unless I broke into his office. A big smile spread across my face. I picked up the phone and called Dave.

"Are you out of your mind?" he said. "I'm not breaking into anyone's office. That place has to have a security system anyway. There's no way we'd ever get away with it. And what would it prove anyway?"

"I'm not sure," I said. "The money is the one thing I can't make any sense of. Look at it this way. Let's assume Melissa or Sharon or any one of the women killed him. How does the money fit in? Or let's assume it was one of the pool players. How does the money fit in with them?"

Dave let out a loud sigh. "I see what you mean," he said. "The only one it really fits with at all is Harry. And that's only if we assume your theory is correct— that he was pressured by Hank to give him money and got fed up."

"But even that theory doesn't satisfy me," I said. "Why would Harry give in to the pressure to begin with? And even if he did, he didn't need to kill him.

That doesn't usually happen unless someone's being blackmailed or bribed."

Dave was silent for a moment. "Blackmail," he said.

"What about it?" I said. "Who would Hank blackmail? We don't have any reason to believe he was doing that."

Dave sighed again. "I don't know," he said. "I think we need more evidence."

I grunted and said good-bye. I was just starting to feel really hopeless when Paul called.

His voice sounded funny. Short of shaky. "Annie, this is Paul," he said. "I just remembered something I think you might be interested in."

"What is it?" I said. "You sound really upset. Are you all right?"

"I have to go," he suddenly whispered. "I'll come to your place." And he hung up.

CHAPTER
13

I nearly went nuts waiting for Paul. I called Dave three times just to ask him what he thought Paul was going to tell me. "I don't know," he screamed the last time I asked. "But I'm coming over. It's the only way I'll ever get you to stop calling me."

Dave was there for over an hour before Paul arrived. We went over my notes together while we waited. Dave agreed with me. The money was the missing link, the odd question that needed to be answered.

When the doorbell rang at 5:45, I jumped. Dave shook his head and got up to answer it. I ran after him.

Paul looked frazzled when I let him in. I asked him to come into the kitchen with us.

"Why'd you hang up so fast? What happened?" I said.

Paul ran his hand through his hair. "I thought I heard someone," he said. "I think someone was listening to me."

81

"Do you know who it was?" Dave asked.

"No," Paul said. "I looked around after I hung up, but I didn't see anybody."

I let out a big sigh. "Tell me what you wanted to talk about before I go out of my mind," I said. "The suspense is killing me."

Paul looked at both of us with a nervous and serious expression. "Remember when you told me when Hank got his first big raise? You said you were sure it was on March 18th because he wanted to celebrate St. Patrick's Day a day late?"

I nodded. "Yes, I remember. What about it?"

"Fred Matthews was missing as of March 17th. That was the day he went to work in the morning and never came home again."

Dave and I looked at each other and frowned. I was still busy thinking about what Paul had said when Dave spoke up. "Are you suggesting that Hank may have killed Fred Matthews?" he asked Paul.

There were beads of sweat on Paul's forehead. "I don't know what to think," he said. Then he hesitated a moment. "There's something else," he said. "March 18th was also the day I paved the parking lot. And I noticed that a part of the lot had been roughed up a bit before I started the paving."

I stared at him.

"There might be a connection there, don't you think?" Paul said.

"Yes," I said. "I do. But I don't know what the connection is. Let's think about this. First, why would Hank kill Fred Matthews?"

Paul shook his head and Dave looked deep in thought. "We already know they had an argument because Jeff Rogers overheard it," Dave said. "We don't know what it was about. But let's assume it was over something really big. Something that really mattered to both of them. Their fight could have gotten violent enough that Hank ended up killing Fred. He may not have meant to. It might have been an accident."

"But then why wouldn't Rogers have known about it?" Paul said. "He was there during the fight. If Hank killed Matthews, it would have to have been after Rogers was gone."

"Maybe Rogers does know about it," Dave said. "And maybe he has a reason to keep quiet about it."

"But then who killed Hank?" I said. "I don't want you to think I don't care about Fred Matthews. But it's Hank's murder I need to solve right now."

Dave gave me a patient little smile. "I know," he said, "but what Paul is suggesting is that the two murders may be connected. I think he may be right."

I wrinkled my brow and stared at them. "But how?" I said. "How could they be connected?"

"I don't know," Dave said. He was beginning to sound impatient. "We have to come up with some theories."

I nodded. "Well, what if Hank got all that money from Fred Matthews? What if he killed him and then stole it from him?"

Paul's eyes opened wide. "I guess that's possible," he said. Then he frowned. "But it still doesn't explain who killed Hank."

"Well, maybe someone saw Hank kill Matthews, and then they blackmailed Hank," I said.

Dave's eyebrows shot up. "I like that," he said. "That's good. Real good. So Hank kills Matthews, someone witnesses it and blackmails him. But Hank was the one with all the money. If he was paying someone off, why would he have so much money?"

"Because he took so much from Matthews that he had plenty left over?" Paul suggested.

Dave pursed his lips. "Why would Fred Matthews have so much money on him?" Dave said.

Paul looked stumped. "I don't know," he said.

We were all silent for a few minutes. Then I got an idea. "Would Rogers still be at the site?" I asked Paul.

Paul looked at his watch. "He might be," he said. "He usually stays late to do paperwork."

I asked Paul for the number and dialed. Rogers answered on the first ring. "Jeff, this is Annie Johnson," I said. "Remember when you told us about the fight between Hank and Fred Matthews? Can you remember anything at all that either of them said?"

There was a long pause. "No," Jeff finally said, "I can't. Is there anything more?"

I was a little annoyed by his attitude but I tried not to show it. "Were you there during the whole fight?" I said.

When he didn't answer, I went on. "The reason I'm asking is that Fred Matthews was reported missing the very next day. He never came home that night. We were wondering if Hank might have killed him by accident during their fight."

There was another slight pause. "I don't know what went on after I left," he said. "They seemed to have calmed down, but they were still there when I went home. I suppose they could have started up again after I left. Anything's possible."

"Okay," I said. "Thanks, Jeff."

After I hung up, I told Dave and Paul what Rogers

had said. "There's only one thing wrong with that theory," Dave said. "Matthews called Rogers the next day and told him he was quitting. So Hank couldn't have killed him that night."

I made a face at Dave and called Rogers back. "Sorry, it's me again," I said when Rogers barked into the phone. "I just want to ask about Matthews calling in to quit. You said he called the next day. So it was the day after the fight. Do you know where he was calling from? And can you remember what time it was?"

"I have no idea where he called from," Rogers said in an even tone. "I assumed it was from home. And I can't remember the time of day. I think it was sometime before lunch."

"Thanks, Jeff. I promise not to bother you anymore tonight." He hung up without a word.

"Well, that blows that theory," Dave said when I repeated what Jeff told me.

"Assuming Jeff is telling the truth," I said. "We have no reason to know that he is."

Paul stared at me with his mouth open. Dave was nodding his head. "Paul," Dave said, "tell us everything you can remember about what happened on March 17th and the days after. I want to know everything. When the police came, when Matthews' wife came, what they said, who they talked to. Everything you can think of."

"And include things that don't necessarily seem important to you," I said. "You never know what will tie everything together."

We spent the next hour listening to Paul and asking each other questions. When we were finished, I was pretty sure I knew what had happened. We just needed to visit the site and check it out.

"Do you think Jeff is still there?" I said to Paul.

"He could be," he said. "I've heard he stays pretty late sometimes. He could be there until midnight for all I know."

"Why don't you just call him?" Dave said. "That way we'll know for sure."

"I already told him I wouldn't call anymore tonight," I said.

Dave rolled his eyes. "Then give me the phone. I'll do it."

Dave picked up my phone and dialed. He let it ring at least a dozen times before he hung up. "He's gone home," Dave said. "Come on. Let's go."

Paul looked scared to death. He didn't move. Dave had to lift him from his chair by his arms and practically drag him to the car.

CHAPTER 14

It was past eight when we arrived at the site. The entrance gate was locked and Paul had to open it for us. That alone took almost ten minutes. I was so nervous I couldn't stand it. Anyone driving by could have seen us. And I was worried about setting off an alarm.

"Forget about that," Dave kept telling me. "If the police come, we have a good explanation for being here."

I laughed. "Oh, yeah. And as soon as they find out who I am, they'll be happy to let us go. After all, I'm such a fine, upstanding citizen as far as they're concerned."

Dave laughed a little and put his arm around me. "Don't worry," he said. "I have a feeling this will all be over very soon."

Once we got inside the gate, we parked Dave's car in the back. That way it would be out of sight. Paul let us in the back entrance. We stood near the doorway until Paul turned on the lights.

"Someone's going to see us and call the police," I said.

"It's just until I find the key to the backhoe," Paul said. "Then I'll turn the lights off again."

When Dave started to follow Paul, I grabbed his arm. "Stay here with me," I said. "I don't want to go in there."

Dave shook his head and smiled. Then he put his arm around my shoulder. He kept it there until Paul got back.

"Did you find them?" I said.

Paul jangled a set of keys. "Right here," he said. "I've only operated the backhoe a few times, so I'm not sure which key fits. But I know it's here."

Paul turned out the lights and locked the door. Then we walked toward the east side of the lot where the heavy equipment was kept. I can't tell a backhoe from a wheelbarrow so I just followed along. Paul walked over to a big yellow thing and got in. He tried a few keys but they didn't work.

I kept looking around to see if anyone had spotted us. Every noise I heard made me jump. I was sure I heard footsteps at one point. I whirled around and tried to see in the darkness. My night vision is bad, and there were no lights on in the lot. I couldn't see a thing.

"What's the matter?" Dave whispered.

"I thought I heard someone," I said.

He shook his head. "You're just imagining things. Calm down, will you?"

I was about to give him a smart answer when we both heard a loud noise. Paul had finally gotten the backhoe started.

"Do you want to come along for the ride?" Paul yelled down to us.

I looked at Dave. "I'm not staying out here," I said. "Let's get in."

Paul waited until we had jammed ourselves in next to him. It wasn't comfortable. But it felt a lot safer being protected by the machine than standing out there in the open.

"Okay," Paul said. "Here goes."

"Do you remember the exact spot where the ground was roughed up?" Dave asked.

"No," Paul said. "But I'm pretty sure of the general area. It was somewhere over here."

Paul started to break up the asphalt as best he could. It wasn't an easy job, though. I don't think the equipment was designed for it. It was almost an hour before he had broken up the surface and moved some of the pieces. Then he was able to start digging underneath. By that point, I was sick to my stomach. The backhoe shook us up an awful lot. And I was terrified of being caught. I wasn't sure what worried me most—being caught by the police or being caught by the killer.

"I can't find anything," Paul was saying. "It's so hard to see with these lights. They don't shine directly on the ground."

"Maybe I should get out," Dave said. "I could get a closer look."

"No," I said as I grabbed his arm. "Stay here."

Dave gave me an exasperated look. "Annie, calm down. You're getting hysterical. There's no one here. I'm perfectly safe and so are you."

I still didn't let go of his arm. He pried my fingers

loose. Then he opened the door and hopped out. I quickly pulled it shut and started to shiver.

"Don't worry," Paul said. "He'll be all right."

Paul began to dig again. He stopped every so often to yell down to Dave. The response was always the same. Dave had seen nothing yet. Not a single clue. I was beginning to think we were wasting our time.

By that time Paul had cleared away most of the asphalt and shoved it into a large pile over to one side. That left a rather large area where the bare ground was exposed. Then Paul started to dig trenches. He began at one side and dug a trench about fifteen feet long. When Dave shook his head, he started on another patch. The procedure went on for close to an hour. Then suddenly Dave put up his hand.

Paul stopped and shouted down, "What do you see?"

"I'm not sure," Dave said. "But it looks like we've found something. Keep going."

I started to shake again. "Do you really think he could have buried him under the asphalt?" I said.

"I know it sounds gruesome," Paul said. "But yes, I do. I'm assuming he was already dead before he put him here."

I shuddered and looked away. "Sorry," Paul said. He started a trench next to the last one when Dave started to wave at us.

"What is it?" Paul yelled.

Dave didn't answer right away. He came over to the backhoe and got back inside. He looked a little pale. When he spoke, his voice was very unsteady. "I think I saw a hand," he said.

"Oh, my God," I said.

Paul was about to jump out when I saw something move. I grabbed Paul's arm.

"Someone's out there," I said. Paul closed the door. I closed the side window.

"Let's just wait and see what happens," Paul said.

I'm still not sure that was a good idea. But I don't know what would have worked better. A moment after Paul spoke, we heard a gunshot. The bullet missed us in the cab and hit the hoe.

"Someone's shooting at us," I screeched.

"Get down," Dave said as he pushed my head toward the floor. Paul crawled to the floor and Dave took his place. He stayed upright and started moving the backhoe.

"What are you doing?" I yelled. "You're going to get killed. Get down."

"This thing isn't bullet-proof," Dave said. "This is our only chance."

I was frantic by that time and I started crying. Paul wasn't moving an inch. I think he was as scared as I was.

Dave, on the other hand, seemed to be fearless. He started moving the controls and driving the backhoe forward. We heard another shot—and another—and another. Dave just kept driving as the bullets glanced off the cab and the hoe. Luckily for us, the man was shooting wildly and Dave was not hit.

Suddenly we heard the backhoe crunch against the building. At the same time a scream of pain and anger came from right next to the cab.

"It's okay," Dave yelled. "We're safe." Then he grabbed Paul by the collar. "I need your help," he said. "Now!"

Dave and Paul jumped out and I watched. Jeff Rogers was pinned between the building and the backhoe. His right arm was held behind him and above his head at an unnatural angle. His gun was on the ground. He was trembling and crying even more than I had been. It served him right. He'd killed two men and tried to frame me for one of the murders.

Paul and Dave had little trouble controlling Rogers until the police came. Dave held the gun on him while Paul made the call. After the police arrived, Dave showed them where to dig. In less than ten minutes they had uncovered Fred Matthews' body.

*   *   *

Dave, Paul, and I spent a good part of the night in the police station. We each gave separate statements. And the police took a long time with each one of us. As we were leaving, Detective Foster waved me over. He was the one who had threatened to charge me with Hank's murder. He didn't apologize. I hadn't really expected him to. But his expression was humble and he was kind.

"We'll let you know what happens," he promised me. "Now get some sleep. You've had a long night."

I gave him a grateful and forgiving smile as I said good-bye.

As it turned out, Dave and I had figured it right. We read all about it in the newspapers for days afterwards. It was Jeff Rogers who'd had the argument with Fred Matthews. He'd caught Matthews stealing money. Matthews tried to deny it and Rogers fired him. Matthews became furious and went after Rogers. They got into a fistfight and it became more violent by the minute. Both of them lost control. When Rogers threw a paperweight at Matthews, it hit him in the head. He hadn't intended to kill him, but it happened. He hit him too hard, and he hit him in the wrong place.

When Rogers realized what he had done, he panicked. He was afraid no one would believe it was an accident. So he decided to hide the body. The parking lot for the building was due to be paved the next day. Rogers used the backhoe and a shovel to dig a hole in a corner of the lot. He buried Matthews in it.

The next morning Paul noticed the area that was not smooth. When he asked Rogers about it, Rogers brushed him off. Then he ordered Paul to get the parking lot paved right away.

That same day, Rogers pretended that Matthews had called in to quit his job without any notice. When the police came, he didn't mention the argument. In fact, he claimed to have seen Matthews leave at quitting time the night before.

What Rogers didn't know until later that day was that Hank had witnessed the whole thing. Hank had heard the argument. Hank had seen the fight. And Hank had seen Fred Matthews die. Hank had watched as Rogers buried Matthews in the lot.

When Hank told Rogers what he knew, Rogers pulled a gun on him. But Hank talked him out of it. Hank convinced him he would get away with Matthews' murder as long as he paid Hank to keep quiet. Hank didn't ask for a lot that first night. That's why Rogers agreed to it. But he kept coming back. And each time he wanted more.

Hank let the whole thing go to his head. He started to feel like he and Rogers were buddies. Like they were in on something big together. He even had me invite Rogers to dinner. That's when Rogers learned where I lived and what my house looked like. I'd insisted on giving him the full tour. I was so proud of the house, even the basement.

Later when Hank asked Rogers for money one too many times, Rogers made a plan. He knew Hank had broken up with me a short time before. I was the perfect suspect—a jilted lover. And he knew where I lived. My basement windows were large enough to get through and the latches were rusty and weak. It took very little to get one open and slide the body through.

Hank had never guessed what was coming, Rogers told the police. He'd agreed to meet Rogers late at night for another payoff. But when Hank showed up, Rogers pulled his gun and used it.

*   *   *

Dave and I were written up in the papers. They made a big deal about our solving two crimes at once without having any formal training. When we stopped in at Barb and Artie's and BJ's Tap, everyone cheered at the top of their lungs. It was a good feeling. Even Amy smiled at me as if she meant it.

Everyone we know thinks we're hotshot detectives. Paul thinks we should get ourselves a couple of PI licenses and open a business. I keep telling him he's crazy. I'll have to admit we did a pretty decent job of figuring it out, though. If another murder comes our way that needs solving, I don't think either of us will hesitate to give it a try.